Delia was melting on the spot

It was unfair that Joe looked s-o-o-o good holding that little baby. He shouldn't have, of course. He should have looked ill at ease and awkward as he cuddled Libby in the crook of his arm. The soft worn jeans, scuffed cowboy boots and Stetson only added to the picture.

Delia sighed. Joe could be married. Or divorced. He could have children somewhere whom he had walked and burped and fed. And loved. And there had to be a woman in his life. Or two. Or more, she thought with a frown, recalling his bad reputation.

His brother had been wild and had died doing some crazy stunt with a car, and his sister was wild in her own way, with a couple of kids and now someone else's husband. *Mine,* Delia thought. *Good luck to them.*

Those Browns, everyone in July, Texas, had said years ago, are nothing but trouble. Well, to look at J. C. Brown now, anyone would think he was Father of the Year.

And as sexy as hell.

Dear Reader,

A few years ago I dragged home a white chipped-paint table
from a local consignment store and put it in the living room.
Now, this particular living room was finally empty of six
teenagers and a mountain of athletic shoes, backpacks
and other messes. (Love you. Bye. Don't forget to e-mail.)
I then decided I hated the old couch, so I dragged it outside.
I sold the dining-room set and the china closet because they
didn't match my beautiful "new" old table. I ripped up all the
carpets and tossed them in the front yard with other pieces
of furniture that I no longer liked. The junk man came and
hauled away everything but my husband, the dog and the
wedding crystal. A new lifestyle was born.

So of course I had to write about a heroine with a chance to
start over with nothing but her clothes and her craft supplies,
a box of country music and a yearning for privacy after
raising someone else's children. Meet Delia Drummond, the
heroine of *The Best Man in Texas*. I hope you like her story.

And look for *Made in Texas* next month, when Adelaide
Larson packs everything she owns—which isn't much—
when she inherits a small fortune and the house of her
dreams. Wherever Addie goes, disaster is sure to follow.

But everyone needs a chance to start over.

Sincerely,

Kristine Rolofson
P.O. Box 323, Peace Dale, RI 02883

KRISTINE ROLOFSON

THE BEST MAN IN TEXAS

HARLEQUIN®

TORONTO • NEW YORK • LONDON
AMSTERDAM • PARIS • SYDNEY • HAMBURG
STOCKHOLM • ATHENS • TOKYO • MILAN • MADRID
PRAGUE • WARSAW • BUDAPEST • AUCKLAND

To Pat and Nancy

ISBN 0-373-69189-0

THE BEST MAN IN TEXAS

Copyright © 2004 by Kristine Rolofson.

www.eHarlequin.com

Printed in U.S.A.

1

"POOR DELIA." The statement was accompanied by a sigh and a shake of Georgia Ball's gray-haired head. "I don't know what she's going to do now."

"I know." Annie took a tissue from her purse, just in case Georgia started crying again. She ignored the curious looks from the bridge group piling into the restaurant for dessert after their weekly game of cards. Everyone in the town of July, Texas, was still gossiping about Delia's divorce, and it wouldn't do to put on a show, not at the Yellow Rose Diner in the middle of the afternoon.

"And the humiliation," Georgia added, lowering her voice as she took the offered tissue.

"It certainly is a shame," Annie agreed, taking a sip of iced tea. "Delia's such a nice girl, and to have had such a hard time of it, breaks my heart, it does."

"I keep telling her that she should move back home," Georgia declared. She was in her early sixties, but she had the energy of a much younger woman and the often-ferocious self-confidence of a teenager. "I have the extra room and there's no reason for Delia to be paying rent somewhere when I sure wouldn't mind the company."

"No," her friend said. "Company would be nice for you, but—"

"And Delia can't afford to keep that house, not now that Martin has it up for sale."

"No, but—"

Georgia frowned over her coffee cup. "But what, Annie?"

"Maybe Delia—" she hesitated, thinking over her next words.

"Maybe Delia *what?*"

"Might want to, um, be by herself. Get her own place. Kick up her heels a bit."

"Why on earth would she want to do that?"

Annie decided it was better not to explain. Georgia Ball wasn't known for her listening ability, but she was a good friend. And there was no sense in trying to explain to a mother that her adult daughter might prefer some privacy. "No reason, I suppose. Just that she raised those children of Martin's and now they're all grown-up and, well, Delia is still young."

"She's thirty-three," her mother declared. "Not exactly a spring chicken."

Annie tried to remember what her own life had been like when she was thirty-three, but all she remembered was a blur of making meat loaf and ironing shirts. "That's a fairly young age for a woman, especially in this day and age."

Georgia shrugged. "That depends on the woman. Delia needs—"

Annie waited. She thought Delia needed a weekend in Las Vegas or a month in Hawaii, and maybe some time with a hunky lifeguard, but she didn't expect Delia's mother to think the same way.

"She needs help," Georgia concluded. "And she shouldn't be living alone, especially not now. It could take her a while to get over the shock."

Annie couldn't argue with that. Having your husband divorce you for a younger woman was shocking enough, but finding out he was in love with the pregnant truck stop waitress only added to the confusion. And the baby, born six months ago, didn't even belong to Martin Drummond. "It's all so unbelievable."

"He told Delia he never meant to fall in love with Julie Brown, but he couldn't help himself. She needed him, he'd said." Georgia rolled her eyes. "The only thing Julie Brown ever needed was birth control."

"Marty was a fool. I never liked him, not even when he was mayor. He was always a little too full of himself, that man was." And to add insult to injury, he wanted to sell his and Delia's house and run off with Julie Brown the very second his youngest child turned eighteen. In a little over eight months, Delia had gone from married and settled to divorced and abandoned. It was downright disastrous, even in this day and age when no one seemed to know better.

"I thought he was too old for her—and I told her that, too, when she started seeing him—but Delia was sure she was in love. She was only twenty when she met him, what did she know about love?" Georgia sighed again and shook her head. "And then she took care of those children after their mother died. All this time I thought Delia had the perfect marriage. They seemed so settled and peaceful-like."

"Thirteen years of marriage is a long time." Annie leaned forward so that no one in the diner could overhear. "I'm almost glad they never had children together. At least Delia is free and clear and never has to see that foolish man again."

"Small comfort," Georgia said. "I guess the good Lord's not going to give me grandchildren after all."

"Lots of women Delia's age get married and start families," Annie said, sorry she'd brought up the subject of Delia's fertility. She hadn't meant to hurt Georgia's feelings. "Really, Georgie, anything could happen."

"Anything *has*," Georgia replied, choking back tears. "My poor sweet Delia has a broken heart."

DELIA KNEW there was something wrong with her, something intrinsically twisted, because she also knew that she was supposed to fall apart, especially after her future ex-husband announced that the house they'd shared for thirteen years was to be sold, the profit—if there was any—divided between them, because he'd fallen in love with another woman and wanted a divorce.

It was the best way, he'd said. Fair to both of them.

Well, Delia had heard herself say, what in the hell does *fair* have to do with anything, huh, Martin?

She knew there was something wrong with her because instead of efficiently emptying her kitchen like some kind of domestic robot, she should be falling apart, collapsing to the white tile floor while she wept and cursed and wondered where she'd left the prescription for the Valium Dr. Arthur had given her. She should toss her wedding china dinner plates to the floor, take scissors to the tuxedo Martin had forgotten to pack, and—after all, because this was Texas—she should then grab her late father's shotgun, drive down the street to the law office parking lot and pelt the tires of Martin's beloved Ford Ranger with bullets.

Except that Martin wasn't there, because he was off vacationing with his young girlfriend. And even if Delia had shot up his car months ago, he wouldn't have pressed charges. Not Martin Michael Drummond. Before he'd become filled with lust for the twenty-five year old waitress who'd served him a Cobb salad at precisely twelve-forty-five every workday, he'd spent his life making sure that everything ran smoothly, his actions bringing only good publicity for his law firm and a life worth smiling about. Come to think of it, Martin's smug smile had aggravated the daylights out of her for a very long time.

And that's how Delia knew that something was wrong, that the odd feeling streaming through her might—just might—be relief. Winds of change, she decided, wishing she could remember what song that phrase came from. Maybe something of Uncle Gin's, she supposed, missing him once again. There was a reading of his will tomorrow, to be tactfully handled by Martin's partner, Delia was certain, as she and Martin hadn't spoken since last month, when they'd appeared in court together.

But the will business was tomorrow and right now she had to decide what to do with two cabinets full of Tupperware. Surely her husband's new girlfriend would have little use for it and, since Delia never intended to cook again, all those convenient containers could be donated to her mother's church for their thrift shop.

Delia eyed the growing stack of boxes destined for charity. Her wedding china would make someone very happy, she supposed. As would the sets of copper-bottomed frying pans and ridiculously expensive French cookware she was surprised Martin hadn't confiscated for his own use. Surely his new town house on the edge of town needed pans that were guaranteed not to burn on the bottom. Or maybe Martin was eating out these days.

Eating out with his new, nubile girlfriend while Delia spent her days and nights emptying closets and packing boxes.

Good riddance to all of it. She felt the same way about the furniture. Wherever she went from here, she wasn't going to drag one single remnant of her married life behind her. And that was another thing

Delia thought was wrong with her: she really didn't mind leaving the house. She didn't mind leaving the furniture, or the responsibility of raising teenagers or the strange boredom she'd fought for years. In fact, Delia wished she could walk away from the kitchen and its neat stacks of labeled and taped cardboard boxes, but before she could make up her mind where to go, her stepdaughter opened the back door and strolled inside the room.

"This place is a mess," Jennifer said, stepping carefully around the boxes to get a glass from the cupboard by the sink. The teenager proceeded to pour herself a glass of orange juice, unaware that some of the juice splattered out of the glass onto the floor.

"Yes," Delia answered, though she privately thought Jennifer was unaware of what a real mess looked like. If she'd wanted to, Delia thought she could have made a pretty decent mess of leaving this house. "Did you come by to get the last of your things?"

"Yeah. I've got a couple of bags of clothes in my room." She sighed and leaned against the tiled counter. "I can't believe you're making Dad sell the house."

"I'm not *making* your father do anything," she said, not for the first time. "We both agreed this was a fair way to settle things." And she didn't add that she didn't have any great desire to live in the sprawling home by herself. It had belonged to her husband—her ex-husband—and his first wife Mary before she'd died and left her husband with three young children to raise. As much as Delia had tried to put her own imprint on the house—she'd tried new paint, flowered wallpaper, filmy white curtains, floral slipcovers—nothing had basically changed the nature of a house designed with open space and entertaining in mind. Sometimes Delia longed for the cozy rooms of her childhood home, for window seats and braided rugs and the battered pine cupboard that housed her mother's good china.

Her next home, whenever she could afford one, would have wood floors. She would have a light-filled studio and plenty of shelves for her beads and fabric. Delia attempted, partly from habit and partly out of habitual politeness, to engage her stepdaughter in conversation. "So, how is everything with you?"

Jennifer, tall and thin, blond and elegant, shrugged. "Fine. This town really bores me to tears."

Delia had heard that same complaint from her for years. "How do you like the new place?"

"It's okay, for a condo. But I'm going off to college in a few weeks, so it doesn't really matter where Dad lives now."

Delia thought it should matter more, but she didn't say anything. It had been hard to raise three stepchildren who thought of her as an unpaid servant, but she'd persisted, knowing that they needed a home and a mother and all the comfort a family could give. It had never quite worked out though. Especially not after they became teenagers and treated

Delia like she was a rug to walk on. Kevin and Karl, the twins, were now twenty-one, about to start their last year of college in California, where they lived year-round now. They'd never had much use for a stepmother, unless it was to buy them clothes or fill the refrigerator. She'd tried getting close to them, but they'd had each other for company. If there was a problem they went to their father, who was pretty good at making problems go away. Too good, Delia had said more than once, as she watched the boys grow up into self-absorbed, spoiled young men.

She really didn't know why Martin had married her after all. Oh, maybe he thought he was in love with her. She'd been too much in love to listen to her mother's warnings about a "ready-made family." So by marrying her, he'd acquired a full-time housekeeper and nanny for his children without having to provide anything but room and board. He'd had sex thrown in for free—okay, she'd enjoyed that, too, up until the last few years when Martin's interest had clearly waned—and she'd gained fifteen pounds out of frustration.

"I should start exercising," she muttered. Those added fifteen pounds were something else to add to the list of what she blamed herself for.

"What?" Jennifer looked up from her perusal of the box of cooking utensils.

"Nothing. Do you need any more boxes? There are plenty on the porch and you take those pans, if you want. You might need them for your own place someday."

"No, I'm all set," the young woman said, taking her juice and her size-seven body toward the hall door. "One more trip for my winter clothes and then I've got everything I need."

So do I, Delia wanted to say. I no longer need a husband who doesn't love me or a house that was never mine or three ungrateful stepchildren who didn't know a good thing when they had it.

What she needed, Delia decided, was a good thing of her own.

J. C. BROWN cursed the town, the buildings, the streets and the people. He cursed the red light at the intersection of Main and Cottonwood and the traffic stalled by a UPS truck that had stopped to make a delivery to Gilroy's Hardware store. He resisted the urge to honk the horn of his own pickup, only because he didn't want to call attention to himself. The last thing he wanted, on this god-awful hot day, was to advertise that he was in July, that another "badass Brown" was driving down Main Street looking for trouble.

And J. C. Brown wasn't looking for trouble. Well, he amended, checking out two twenty-something women smoking cigarettes in front of the Cottonwood Lounge. Maybe he was. He pulled the truck over and parked along the curb while the women watched him. The taller one, a brunette, tossed her cigarette onto the sidewalk and crushed it with the toe of her boot, while the shorter woman shook her blond hair out of her face and adjusted her sunglasses.

Joe stepped out of the truck and walked around the front to the sidewalk. If he'd worn a hat he would have lifted it, just to make them smile, but he wasn't in the mood for flirting. "Ladies," he said.

"Hey," the tall one replied, while the light-haired woman stared. "How's it goin'?"

"I've had better days," he drawled, leaning against the truck's front fender.

"Yeah," she said, pulling another cigarette out of her shoulder bag. "Tell me about it."

"I'm looking for Julie Brown," he said, unwilling to stand on a hot sidewalk and play games with bored women who smelled like beer and smoke. Those days were over. "You seen her around?"

"Not lately."

The shorter woman finally spoke. "You from around here?"

J.C. shrugged. "Used to be."

"I know you." She nodded. "You're Julie Brown's older brother."

He silently cursed the family resemblance: dark curly hair, green eyes, and an easy smile that could charm rattlesnakes, those were the unmistakable characteristics the Browns had inherited from their father. J.C. often wished he'd gotten more of his mother's genes, but leave it to the Brown side to dominate everything in his life, even the DNA.

"But Julie comes in here, right?"

The tall one shrugged again. "Used to, until she ran off with the mayor."

"Former mayor," the other woman corrected, shooting a flirty smile toward J.C. "That sister of yours could corrupt a saint."

"Yeah?" Sweat dripped down his back between his shoulder blades and he wondered if he went into the bar if the women would follow him. He was in no mood for seduction, had no interest in pursuing either the tall gal in the short denim skirt or the yellow-haired one, despite a pair of blue eyes that ordinarily would tempt him into forgetting business.

"Absolutely," Blue Eyes declared, looking him over one more time.

"They still serve burgers in there?" He nodded toward the diner across the street.

"Yeah. Too bad we can't join you, but we have to get back to work. Maybe we'll see you down here later, maybe around nine?" It was obviously an invitation for more than a beer.

"Maybe," he drawled, trying to look flattered. "If you run into Julie anywhere, tell her that her brother's in town and looking for her." Not that his sister wouldn't find out soon enough, even though he wouldn't have minded surprising her. He'd had the pleasing vision of hauling her off a bar stool by grabbing her ponytail and hanging on until she went in the direction he wanted her to go, the way he used to when they were kids and she'd stepped right in the middle of some dirt road he was building with his dented Tonka dump truck.

He'd most likely get arrested for doing that now,

but the expression on his sister's face might almost be worth it.

Almost. He was a fine, upstanding citizen now. And he sure as hell wanted to stay that way.

He hesitated before opening the rough wooden door of the Cottonwood. He wouldn't mind a cold beer, and at the same time he could leave a message for his sister with the bartender. Every bartender within fifty miles knew Julie, according to his mother's phone call last night.

The inside of the Cottonwood was dark and cool, a ceiling fan was whirring overhead and the smell of beer wasn't unpleasant. He glanced around the bar, past the line of barstools and the empty tables to the pool table where a couple of young guys were busy competing with each other. His sister wasn't there, just like he'd been told, and the only woman in the place—a woman with chestnut curls—was perched on a bar stool with her back to him. She had a cute, rounded little ass, he noticed, and then he remembered why he was in town. So he walked behind her and took a seat four stools away. He didn't need another "Aren't you J. C. Brown?" conversation.

Fortunately the bartender was no one he recognized and, after the man set the bottle of beer he'd ordered and a chilled glass in front of him, J.C. decided to pour his drink and wait for a few minutes before mentioning his sister. He wasn't sure what he was going to say, either. It was damn embarrassing, trying to hunt down a woman who had left her kids and run off with a man whose marriage she'd broken up.

This wasn't how he intended to spend his summer.

Yet he couldn't help glancing toward the only woman sharing the bar with him. Maybe she knew Julie, but he sure didn't feel like asking. This particular woman didn't look as if she belonged on a bar stool. She was pretty, with an oval face and the kind of skin that felt like satin. She was drinking something frozen and pink, a strawberry daiquiri, he figured, meaning she wasn't a boozer, not a real one anyway. She was most likely waiting for a girlfriend; she wore khaki shorts and a pink T-shirt that made her look more like a soccer mom than a woman ready for afternoon flirtation or a quickie at the High Cotton Hotel next door.

The bartender kept watching her as if he wasn't at all comfortable, meaning she might be a regular with a reputation for having a bad temper. Or she might be a stranger and the guy was wondering if she would be able to pay up.

She didn't seem the least bit concerned as she drained the last of the drink through a wide straw and smiled at the bartender. "Could I have another one, please?"

"That makes four in twenty minutes," he said, sliding the empty glass off the bar. "You sure?"

"Sure I'm sure," she said, her voice cheerful. "I'm trying to get a life."

"Lady," the young bartender said. "You're not

going to get any kind of a life here. Why don't I pour you a cup of coffee instead?"

"Coffee," she announced, "is for stepmothers."

"O—*kay*," he shrugged. "Another daiquiri it is, then."

Damn, she looked familiar, J.C. mused, studying her face in the dim light of the room. Someone from high school, maybe. Her cheeks were almost as pink as the drink she'd just finished and she looked as if she might have been crying.

Coffee is for stepmothers.

Oh, hell. It was all coming back to him now. Golden brown hair, big hazel eyes, a smile that could light up the gym, a sweet voice in algebra class and class secretary in her junior year. If she was who he thought she was, she was the last woman in July he wanted to run into. Except for her mother, maybe, the old bat who'd taught English at the high school.

Just his luck to have found the one place in town where trouble sat. He would never have expected Delia Ball to be drinking her lunch at the Cottonwood on a Wednesday afternoon. J.C. drank his beer and hoped that the woman was tipsy enough to have trouble focusing on her drinking buddy. The bartender took his time fixing the drink; the noise the blender made almost drowned out the old Hank Williams tune coming from the radio on the shelf above the whiskey bottles. The guys in the back started yelling at each other.

He was afraid she might be crying. Not that he blamed her, but weeping women didn't belong in bars.

"There you go, lady." The bartender set another frozen concoction in front of Delia, who smiled at him.

"Thank you." She took a sip from the straw and then noticed J.C. She seemed surprised that he was looking at her, so he quickly looked away and spun the stool around so he could watch the pool players. They were laughing now and J.C. hoped Delia didn't hear some of their muttered four-letter comments to each other.

"Hey," he called to them. "There's a lady in here."

"Oh, sorry." The scrawny kid with the baseball cap didn't look all that bothered by the warning, but for the next few moments he and his friend kept their voices down and J.C. turned back to the bar.

"I know you," Delia said. "From high school."

"Yeah?" He pretended to be uninterested and hoped the expression on his face could be interpreted as boredom.

She frowned, just a little. "Are you from around here?"

"No." He took the last swallow of his beer and set the empty glass down before reaching into his back pocket for his wallet. He set a five-dollar bill on the counter and slid off the stool.

"But you used to be."

He looked up and noted that those hazel eyes were a little unfocussed. He wondered how much rum was in those drinks. "Yeah."

She swiveled to face him and almost lost her balance. One ringless hand reached for the counter. "But I do know you."

J.C. shook his head. "It's the booze talking, sweetheart."

"I might have had a little too much to drink," she said slowly. "But at least I got out of the house."

He looked for help, but the bartender was leaning against the cash register with his cell phone pressed against his ear and was paying no attention to either one of his customers.

"And," she continued. "I've never been drunk before. It's not that bad, you know. In fact, I like feeling...fizzy." As if to prove it, she took another long sip from the straw.

"Well," he said, attempting to walk past her. "You have a nice day getting out of the house and all."

"It's for sale."

He stopped, which was a mistake. Because if he'd kept walking he could have been out the door in about thirty seconds. "What is?"

"My house."

"I'm sorry to hear that." And truly, he was, because the loss of Delia's house was another sin to set on his sister's doorstep. Now that he was closer to her he could see she wore little makeup and there was a dark smudge on her chin. She didn't look much different than she had years ago, not that he had ever gotten close to her. He would have liked to, though. She'd been shy and bookish, yet in a small town like July she'd been a popular girl. And definitely off limits to the likes of him. He'd never expected she'd end up like this, drunk as a skunk in a cowboy bar.

"You know, I think I've had too much to drink." She pronounced each word very carefully. "I'm not sure I can get off this stool."

"Do you *want* to get off this stool?" He took the hand she offered and his fingers closed around warm fingers.

"I think—" She dropped her sneakered feet to the floor. "I think I'd better try, don't you?"

"Well, uh, maybe you should have some coffee—"

"No." She tilted toward him and he reached out and steadied her, his arm circling her back. "Too boring."

"Hey," the bartender waved, his phone still against his ear. "That'll be twenty-four, seventy-five, honey."

"Right. Money." She sighed, and bent down to pick up a bag that was on the floor. She almost succeeded in toppling them both onto the floor in the process.

"I'll get it." He managed to keep one arm around her waist while he rescued her purse.

"Martin always paid the bills," she muttered, taking the bag from him. She rummaged through it until she pulled out a red wallet. She held it toward J.C. "Could you find the money, please? My fingers don't seem to be working."

He found three ten-dollar bills and left them on the counter, then put the wallet back into her bag. Before he returned it to her, he found a gold key chain with four keys attached, which he held on to. There was no way this woman was driving home. "Where's your car, Delia?"

She gave him an odd look. "You know me?"

"Yeah. Where's your car?"

"In the driveway." She smelled like strawberries, but the Delia he remembered from high school would never have looked as if she was going to pass out.

"Whose driveway?"

"Mine."

J.C. looked toward the bartender, who shrugged. "Can you call a taxi to take the lady home?"

The guy shook his head. "He retired. Moved to Idaho."

"What do you do with drunks then?"

"I call the sheriff and he takes them home."

"Oh, please," Delia begged, her eyes huge as she gazed up at him. "Don't have me locked up."

"No one is going to lock you up, sweetheart," J.C. assured her. "But I sure as hell need to help you get home."

"Home?" Her eyes welled with tears. But to his surprise, she gave him her address. "Four-oh-six Lincoln," she said. "It's too big for me."

J.C. looked at the young bartender for help.

"Three blocks north, corner of Main and Lincoln," the guy explained. "You could walk her home. Maybe."

"It's white," she sighed. "And ugly. I hate the couch."

J.C. tried one more time. "Delia, why don't you let me call a friend for you?"

"*We're* friends," she said, patting J.C.'s hand. "I remember you. I let you copy my answers off the math exam."

"And I appreciated it," he assured her, pocketing the keys. "So I guess I'd better walk you home."

"That would be nice," she said, the words slow and succinct as if she was trying very hard to be coherent. "But I don't want to go there."

"No?" He guided her toward the door. He sure as hell wasn't taking her anywhere else.

"No," she said, but she tightened her grasp of his waist. "It's a horrible place. Too many boxes."

"Right." He hoped she wouldn't pass out on him. "But we should get you there anyway."

She stopped again, and her face lit up as she clearly recognized him. And to his dismay, she turned and hugged him. "I might not remember your name," she said, slurring her words a bit. "But I'm glad you came home."

2

"JOE," THE MAN TOLD HER. "Call me Joe."

He was tall, much taller than Martin. Her nose was against his shirt, the scent from the smooth cotton familiar. He used the same fabric softener she did, a comforting thought for someone who had spent most of her adult life doing laundry.

"Joe?" She tried out the name, but it didn't fit the memory of algebra class and the dark-haired boy who had been seated behind her. "No," she said. "That's not right." She blinked against the harsh sunlight when he shoved open Cottonwood's front door and realized she didn't know where she was going once she stepped outside. Or with whom. Not that it mattered, she guessed, since she couldn't get anywhere by herself. She twisted to look up into his face.

"Hey, don't let go of me now," he said, in a low voice that sounded both amused and protective. "You could end up facedown on the sidewalk before I can get you home."

Once again in a short period of time, Delia realized she'd made a mistake. Sucking down four daiquiris in record time hadn't been a good plan at all. She would have to make a list, cataloguing everything she'd done wrong in the past months, but for now she needed to remember how to move her feet in a forward motion.

She didn't want to go home. She didn't want to face the boxes and the empty rooms and the inevitable evening phone call from her mother, who would act as if Delia's life had come to an end and recite all the reasons that Delia shouldn't be depressed.

She wasn't depressed. She was angry. At herself, mostly. She'd wasted the best years of her life and here she was, hanging on to a guy named Joe and staggering out of a bar in broad daylight.

Clearly alcohol wasn't going to be the answer to her divorce problems.

"Steady," he said. "We're going to move to the right and let these kids pass us."

Three teenagers giggled at them and walked past as Delia tried to look sober. Her face was numb, her lips tingled and she couldn't feel her knees, but she figured as long as she could walk and talk she must be okay.

"Good. Don't know them," she whispered.

"What?"

She looked up into a pair of green eyes that crinkled at the corners with an amused expression that was vaguely familiar.

"Small town," she managed to say despite a tongue that didn't seem to want to form words.

"Yeah," he muttered. "Tell me about it."

"Sunglasses," she said, reaching for the purse that dangled from a shoulder strap.

"Just keep walking." His arm tightened around her waist. "We're going to cross the street soon and find your house."

"Can't," she said, the heat making her feel as if she was going to be sick. He leaned her against the window of the Sew Good craft shop while he tried to find her glasses.

And with that, Delia closed her eyes and gave in to the rum.

GEORGIA HUNG UP the phone and reached for her blood pressure machine. If she hadn't skyrocketed to one-sixty it would be a miracle. She'd had three phone calls in the last hour and despite calling Delia five—no, six times, there'd been no answer from that daughter of hers.

Which meant the rumors of Delia's drunken escapade at the old Cottonwood, a place that should have been closed down years ago, could be true.

Which, of course, they just couldn't be. Georgia knew her daughter, had brought her up to be a lady. Not that it had been difficult, not with a lovely girl like Delia, who listened to her parents most of the time and did her homework as if she enjoyed it. She had been the perfect daughter from the day she was born. Oh, she was no beauty, not in a Miss America way, but she had always been such a pretty girl. With such nice manners and a cheerful personality.

Cheerfulness was underrated these days, with all the attention on skinny legs and big artificial breasts and belly button rings. She didn't understand why women wanted to strut around exposing their bellies, but she was grateful that Delia wasn't one of them. Delia, thank goodness, had always been sensible. Even marrying Martin hadn't exactly been an act of rebellion. Delia had been in love and had sworn she knew what she wanted.

Georgia waited the required amount of minutes to determine her pressure, only to discover that she was fine. A little above average, but it was early evening and certainly not unusual to have a slight rise in the numbers. And she knew she shouldn't barge over to Delia's house on the basis of a rumor. Delia was a little depressed these days and didn't need to know that folks in town were wondering if the divorce was turning her into a lush.

She wanted to call her, wanted to hear Delia's calm voice on the other end of the phone, just to reassure herself that all was well. But when Delia didn't answer her phone after seven rings, she called Annie.

"I need you to do me a favor," she said, right after Annie picked up the phone.

"Georgia? What's wrong?" The television news blasted in the background, but soon quieted after Georgia assumed Annie found her remote.

"Look across the street and see if Delia's car is there."

"Why?"

"Because she's not answering her phone." She didn't want to talk about what she'd heard. One shouldn't spread rumors about one's own daughter, after all, not even to one's best friend.

"Maybe she had it disconnected."

"She wouldn't do that. Not without telling me. Just go look, will you, Annie? Please?"

"Hold on," she said. "I'm walking to the window now." There was a pause, then, "Her car's there. I think it's been there all day."

"Are there lights on in the house?"

"It's not dark out, Georgia. I can't tell."

"Well," she stalled, wondering how else she could find out if Delia was home and not out gallivanting with a strange man. "Does it look like she's home?"

"You want me to go over and knock on the door?"

Georgia wanted to say yes, but she realized she was being ridiculous. Spying on Delia was not something that her daughter would easily forgive. "No. I guess I'm just being overprotective. Delia wouldn't be—Delia must be packing. Or taking a shower."

"Or maybe she's gone out with a friend for supper. She wouldn't be cooking, not with all that packing she's doing."

"You're right." Annie made perfect sense, of course. "Her friends have been very helpful that way, keeping her busy and making sure she doesn't spend too much time alone. But—"

"But you want me to call you if I see her come home."

"Well, yes." She tried to laugh at herself, but the sound was more like a sob. "I just hate thinking of what she's going through, Annie. And there's nothing I can do to help."

"You can stop worrying," Annie suggested. "You're going to make yourself crazy. When Louella got divorced I thought she'd never be happy again, and what happened? She met a nice man a year later and now they're living in Houston, happy as can be."

"Call me later," Georgia said, ignoring Annie's comment about her oldest girl. Georgia didn't want Delia meeting any other men or moving to Houston. At least not right away. She wanted her daughter to be *happy*, for heaven's sake, not saddled with another man to take care of.

WELL, JOE SUPPOSED he was stuck taking care of Delia now. At least until he knew she was going to be okay. It would be just his luck to have her succumb to alcohol poisoning while he was the one responsible for her. He cursed again, more at his sister than himself this time. Julie should have been the one cleaning up the mess she made when she'd run away with that Drummond jerk, not Delia.

He'd carried Delia the remaining blocks to her home and even managed to revive Delia long enough to walk her to her kitchen door and unlock it.

He then lay her down on the floor, afraid to sit her

in one of those cane and metal kitchen chairs for fear she'd tip right out and bang her head on the tile floor. He looked for a pillow to tuck under her head and eventually found one in what seemed to be the master bedroom, a room that housed nothing but an oversize dresser, stacks of cardboard boxes and a king-size bed.

He took his time going back to the kitchen. The house was huge, empty and very, very white. Ivory carpet, white walls, large windows and—thank God—very efficient central air conditioning. Another block in that heat and he'd have passed out along with Delia and, with his luck, they'd both have been run over by a cop car.

"Hey, sweetheart," he said, lifting Delia's head in order to slide a pillow under it. The pillowcase was decorated with tiny embroidered blue birds and Delia smiled when her cheek touched it. Her skin felt as soft as he'd expected, but Joe didn't waste any time thinking about that luscious little mouth of hers or the way her T-shirt concealed what looked to be a damn good figure.

No, he had better things to do, like sober the woman up so she could throw him out and he could continue on with what he hoped would be the shortest family reunion in July history.

Ten minutes later he returned with a steaming mug of black coffee. Sitting down beside her, he shook her shoulder as much as he dared and was relieved to see her eyes open. "What on *earth* do you want?" she asked, as clearly as if he was a child who had awakened her from a nap.

"I want you to sober up," he informed her. He held out the mug. "Drink this."

"What's in it?"

"Coffee." It hadn't been hard to make, since the coffeemaker was the only thing left on the kitchen counter. He'd found filters on top of a boxful of spices, and coffee in a tin in the freezer. "Can you sit up?"

"Of course I—" She stopped suddenly as she attempted to sit up. Her wince of pain made Joe feel guilty, though he didn't know why. "Give me a minute."

"Sure." He held on to the mug, and waited for Delia to prop herself against the wall next to a chrome and glass-topped table.

"Okay," she said, reaching for the mug. "Thanks."

"You're welcome."

She took several careful sips. "Well, this has been an interesting day."

"Are you feeling better?"

"I think so. The rum—and the heat," she said, wincing again. "Bad combination."

"Your little, uh, nap seems to have helped."

"I feel better," she admitted. "I'm not used to drinking that much alcohol so quickly. I don't remember how I got here."

"You walked," he said. "Until you passed out."

"I'm sorry."

"It's okay. You're not that heavy."

"We do know each other, don't we? I didn't imagine that?"

"No, we know each other." *I sat behind you in algebra. Alphabetical order: Ashton, Ball, Brown, Carter. You smiled at me every morning. You blushed when I told you that you looked like a candy cane the day you wore a striped sweater to school. I grinned like a fool all day.*

"I remember you from high school," she said, taking another sip of coffee.

"Yeah, but I don't remember cheating off your math papers."

"It's okay. I didn't mind. I wasn't that good in math, so I don't think I would have helped you very much." She smiled, a stunning smile that made his heart jump. He had no business sitting on Delia Drummond's kitchen floor and letting her smile at him.

"Look," he began, about to confess that he was the older brother of the woman who'd stolen her husband. "I have to—"

"Please excuse the mess around here," she said, waving one hand toward the stack of boxes by the back door. "I'm in the middle of moving and the house is up for sale."

"I saw the sign on the lawn." She seemed to be feeling better, he noticed. He could leave now with a clear conscience and go back to what he'd been doing before he walked into the Cottonwood.

"You don't have to look so guilty." Her smile didn't quite light up her eyes this time. "None of this is your fault."

"My sister—" He paused, not knowing what to say. *My sister saw a good opportunity and made the most of it by seducing one of the richest guys in town.*

"Ran off with my husband." Delia's voice was steady, but Joe wondered if that was still the alcohol working. "I've seen her a few times. She's very tall. And beautiful."

"Looks are deceiving."

"Yes, well," her voice trailed off and she glanced around the kitchen as if seeing it for the first time. "I'll be glad to get out of here."

That surprised him. "I would have thought you'd be, uh, upset."

She shook her head. "This was Martin's house, not mine. He was married before, they had three children, then his wife died. It's always been a lot to take care of."

"Where are you going from here?"

Delia took another sip of coffee before answering. "I haven't decided."

Joe didn't point out that it looked like she was running out of time. Maybe she planned to camp out here until the place actually sold, since he didn't think there were too many people in July who could afford a house as large as this one. He'd even spotted a deck and a pool in the backyard.

"I can't seem to decide anything," she confessed. "It's a little embarrassing. I can't seem to figure out what to do next."

"You're not the one who should be embarrassed,"

he said. "Julie shouldn't have been messing around with a married man."

"She's welcome to him," Delia said. "I'm about to start a new life after the fastest divorce in Texas. Sometimes it pays to be married to an attorney." She paused for a moment. "Would you like to have wild and crazy sex in the pool?"

"Drink your coffee, sweetheart." Lord help him, the offer was tempting.

She giggled and did as she was told. "I've never said that to anyone before."

"You might want to, uh, be a little more careful with the booze," he stammered. She laughed again, then as Joe watched in horror, tears welled in her eyes and rolled down her flushed cheeks.

"J. C. Brown," Delia said, trying to catch her breath as she choked back a laugh. "You're blushing."

"Yeah? Well, so are you." He never blushed. It was just hotter than hell outside and he'd hauled a drunk woman six blocks in the afternoon sun, that was all. "And that tells me you haven't had a lot of wild and crazy sex with Martin Drummond."

"You're right." Her eyes were huge. "I'm going to change all that. I have a lot of catching up to do."

"Well, don't look at me." He didn't mean it. He would have liked to topple her onto the tile floor— or, better yet, carry her down that endless hallway to the oversize bed where he'd found the pillows—and make love to her for three or four hours. He knew he could make her smile. And blush.

"I have to get better at this," she declared. "If I'm going to have any kind of interesting life at all."

"Good luck." He needed some air. He needed to get away from a woman who would be very appealing if she wasn't drunk, sleepy and getting kicked out of her house because his sister couldn't keep her legs together. Joe looked at his watch and realized he never did get that lunch at the diner. And he was no closer to finding Julie and talking sense into her, either. He stood and looked down at Delia. "I'm leaving now. You might try to make it to your bed before you fall asleep again."

"Good idea." She smiled. "Thanks again for the help getting home."

"No problem. Take care of yourself."

"I intend to from now on."

Her smile almost got to him, but Joe turned and practically ran out the door. He cursed under his breath when he stepped outside into the hot sun and realized his car was still parked in front of the Cottonwood, six blocks away.

Welcome home.

"Delia!"

The voice penetrated through the pain throbbing in Delia's head. The sound, *Deeeel-yah*, shattered right through a dream she was having about sleeping on a sidewalk while Martin and his girlfriend drove by in a convertible singing "All My Exes Live in Texas."

Deeeel-yah!

She shoved her head underneath a pillow, but the sound only became louder.

"Are you sick, darling?"

Delia rolled over onto her back and tried to open her eyes. "Mom?"

"Who else?" Georgia stomped over to the window and yanked open the drapes, letting bright sun angle over the bed. Delia closed her eyes and moaned.

"What's the matter with you? We're supposed to be at the lawyer's office at eleven o'clock."

She'd almost forgotten about the reading of Uncle Gin's will. It had been delayed for a week because no one could find the papers when the secretary had left because her daughter had an emergency C-section and her grandchild was born six weeks early.

"What time is it now?" She couldn't believe she'd slept so late, but then again, she couldn't believe she'd gotten drunk yesterday afternoon, either.

"A little after nine."

"Nine?"

"I'm early, so shoot me. I thought we might need some time to talk."

"Talk? About the will?" Her head ached, her tongue felt like a bathroom sponge and her stomach was queasy. She would never, ever drink strawberry daiquiris again. Not on a hot afternoon and not four in a row. And not the day before she had to settle the estate of a sweet old great-uncle.

She really didn't like how the summer was starting off.

"I brought doughnuts," Georgia said, ignoring the question. "Should I make some coffee?"

"That would be a good idea." In order to make coffee her mother would have to disappear into the kitchen, easily fifty feet away, leaving the master bedroom in blessed silence.

"I hope you'll use the time to shower."

"I am not giving you a key to my next house."

"The back door was unlocked," Georgia informed her. "I didn't have to resort to using my key."

"I'll have to get a guard dog," she muttered. She waited a moment until she was certain her mother was gone before dragging her body out of the bed. It was a ridiculous bed for one person. Way too big and lonely. Much too empty. J. C. Brown's long, lean body would have filled it nicely, she thought, cringing at the memory of trying to seduce him. She would have to learn how to hold her liquor. She would have to learn how to date again. She stripped off her nightgown and looked at herself in the closet mirror.

And she would have to start doing sit-ups, give up French fries and never, ever eat ice cream again.

Thirty minutes later, Delia decided that she didn't feel too bad after all. Aspirin, a hot shower, makeup and clean hair made her feel as if she could face the day—and her mother—with her customary calm. Once her mother handed her a cup of coffee and put a box of glazed doughnuts on the table, Delia decided that yesterday hadn't been that bad after all.

"Now," Georgia began, sitting down across the table. "Please tell me you weren't in the Cottonwood yesterday afternoon."

"News travels fast." She took a bite of doughnut. Maybe choking on fried dough would divert her mother from pursuing this line of interrogation.

"Oh, please." Georgia rolled her eyes. "Whatever possessed you?"

"Oh, I don't know. The divorce. Packing. A visit from Jennifer. The fact that my life is—"

"You've always been such a good girl," her mother interrupted. "I don't know what I'm going to do with you. There was talk—" She paused and Delia took advantage of the lull and helped herself to another doughnut.

"You were seen," her mother said, "staggering down the sidewalk with a *man*."

She pronounced "man" as if it was a dirty word. And Delia didn't much like the "staggering" description either. "Yes."

"*Yes?*"

"The man—a very good-looking man, by the way—brought me home."

Her mother gasped. "I don't want to hear this."

"It's not as terrible as you think," Delia said. "Unfortunately."

Georgia sighed. "Well, I suppose I'll have to take your word for it. But I hope that you're not sinking into a bad lifestyle." She stood and brought the carafe back to the table to refill the coffee.

"You make it sound as if I'm going to hell."

"Well, I suppose you're entitled to a little lapse in judgment after all you've been through." She returned the pot to the counter and then sat down across from Delia and smiled. "This is nice, isn't it?"

"What is?" She knew exactly what was coming, another suggestion that she move in with her mother to live and die happily ever after.

"Us. Having breakfast together. We'd do just fine, the two of us. I have that big house and you need a place to live and we're family, after all. Two women against the world."

"I told you, Mom, I'm thinking of getting my own place."

"With what? I thought you said Martin mortgaged the house for the kids' college tuition."

"He did, but there might be a little something left over, after the house sells." And the rat had fought against even doing that. The judge hadn't been sympathetic to Delia. He'd just divorced his third wife and was close to bankruptcy because he spent too much time in Vegas. So, the alimony was meager and Delia had too much pride to protest. After all, she ought to be able to take care of herself from now on. Delia's lawyer, a young woman from Austin, had done everything but throw a fit in the middle of the courtroom, to no avail.

"Think how much money you'll save living with me," Georgia pointed out.

At the expense of her sanity, not to mention her

pride, Delia thought, but she sipped her coffee and thought about looking in the classifieds for a place to rent. She wouldn't need much, just a bed, a bathroom and a gas oven to stick her head into whenever the prospect of living with her mother became too much to bear.

THE LAST WILL and testament of Horatio Guinness was a simple document, handwritten by him on the back of a piece of sheet music and spattered with something that looked like chili sauce.

Delia blinked back tears. Horatio had just loved chili.

At the brief meeting, no one contested the old man's scribbled wishes. It wasn't as if Georgia wanted her uncle's old guitars or boxes of papers; even if she was the least bit sentimental, which she insisted she wasn't, she wouldn't have known what to do with a mobile home filled with things that smelled like cigars, whiskey and onions. Heck, she said, everyone assumed he rented the place and the only thing he owned was that old truck and a couple of guitars.

There was no other family to protest the fact that Uncle Horatio left all his worldly possessions to his great-niece, which meant that the old man's wishes would be respected. At least that's what Martin's partner, recently divorced and the recent owner of a Ferrari, had told Delia this morning. He'd wished her luck and hinted that he'd be glad to take her out for drinks some night.

Delia had pretended she hadn't heard him. She'd followed her mother out of the downtown law office and driven them both to the Pecan Hollow Mobile Home Park, five and a half miles north of town.

"What a job we've got ahead of us," Georgia said, surveying the cluttered interior of the trailer. "Maybe we should find someone to haul the whole mess to the dump. That'd be the easiest thing to do with all this junk."

"I think I should go through everything first." Delia peered into the bedroom. Her great-uncle's double bed was neatly covered with a patchwork quilt as if he had straightened it before dying of a heart attack while frying his morning eggs. "I can't just throw it all away."

"I suppose not, but you've got enough to do right now, with having to sell the house and dealing with the divorce. Horatio would understand." Georgia fanned herself with her hand. "It's too hot in here. I'm going to step outside. That onion smell—"

"I know." Delia suspected that her uncle put fried onions in every meal he ever cooked, including breakfast. Horatio was partial to freshly chopped onions on top of his eggs, along with crackers, chopped peppers and a big chunk of cheddar cheese. "You'd think after all this time the smell wouldn't be so strong."

"If you're going to work in here, you'd better get the air conditioning fixed."

"Yes." They'd realized almost immediately that

the unit wasn't working. Delia had fiddled with the thermostat and nothing happened, though the electricity worked. She'd have to remember to bring a fan next time. Delia opened the narrow closet door she hoped contained the air-conditioning unit, but the space was piled high with sheet music. Uncle Gin's career as a songwriter had ended decades ago, but it looked like he had kept on writing. "What am I going to do with his music?"

"Oh, Lord," Georgia said, climbing down the metal stairs. "I thought he got rid of that stuff years ago."

"Or else he just kept writing more," Delia replied, lifting the top paper to see for herself. There were stacks of sheet music, notes and even some scraps of paper with lyrics scribbled in Horatio's shaky script. The country singer known as "Gin" Guinness had achieved some fame as a songwriter years before when he lived in Austin, but he'd never hit the big time. And he'd never been much of a businessman, which was why he'd spent the last thirty-two years of his life in Pecan Hollow. "I can't throw this away."

"What else would you do with it?"

"I don't know, but I can't just toss it out. Someone might want these songs someday."

"The heat's gotten to you, honey. Let's go out for a nice lunch," Georgia said from outside. "I could drink a gallon of iced tea right about now with a piece of Key lime pie for dessert."

"All right." But she would return later on, if only

to read the song on the top of the closest box called,
"I've Got All Night to Love You But The Dog Needs
Me More."

3

"HEARD J. C. BROWN is back in town," the waitress at the Yellow Rose announced after she put their glasses of iced tea on the table. She gave Delia a sly look, which didn't go over well with Georgia. What on earth was that all about?

Delia didn't answer and acted completely unimpressed with Mary Lou's announcement, but Georgia knew she had to keep a close eye on her daughter. This drinking thing yesterday wasn't good. And she knew darn well that Delia was hungover. Those dark circles under her eyes and the way she squinted when she took off her sunglasses were a dead giveaway. As soon as Mary Lou, class of 1981 and girl voted "Most Likely To Succeed" took their order and moved away, Georgia leaned forward.

"That Brown boy was in high school with you, wasn't he?"

"Yes," Delia said, but to Georgia's horror, she blushed. "He was probably in one of your English classes."

"Hmm." She might recall a quiet, tall young man

who attracted lots of attention from silly girls and was rumored to be wild, though Georgia didn't remember any of that nonsense—not that she would have put up with it for one minute in her classroom, of course. "Didn't he have an older brother?"

"He died in a car accident years ago."

"That's right." She couldn't believe how bad her memory was getting. "And the sister—oh, good heavens, Delia," Georgia said. "Don't tell me that *Julie* Brown is related to—"

"Yes." She took a long drink of tea before adding, "She's the sister."

"Nothing but trouble, all of them," Georgia said, sipping at her own drink. There were a lot of Browns in the county, enough so it was a common name. And truth be told, she hadn't wanted to hear anything about Martin's girlfriend. No other woman could hold a candle to Delia. She wished they'd hurry up with the chicken salad. At this rate she'd have been better off at the Burger Barn. "Good Lord, I'm hungry."

"I saw J.C.—Joe—in the bar yesterday," Delia said, as casually as if she'd announced she got a good deal on paper towels at Wal-Mart.

"Oh, please don't tell me—" Suddenly the stories she'd heard yesterday made perfect, horrible sense.

"Yes, he was the person who brought me home and yes, he was a complete gentleman the entire time." Delia moved her glass to the side when that snoopy waitress brought their lunch plates.

"Oh, my," was all Georgia could reply. Annie had said she hadn't seen a thing, which meant she'd been watching *Everybody Loves Raymond* repeats instead of the house across the street. Annie was slipping, bless her heart.

"Enjoy your lunch," Mary Lou said. "I'll bring refills on the tea in a minute."

"No hurry," Delia said, reaching for the ketchup. The girl always loved to put ketchup on her hamburgers. It was nice to see that some things didn't change. Or maybe outwardly Delia looked fine—except for those dark shadows—but inside she was falling apart.

"You know, dear," Georgia whispered, her mound of chicken salad forgotten. "Maybe you should, ah, see someone."

"See someone? About what?" Delia attacked her hamburger with the ferocity of a bear fresh out of the winter cave.

"You have a right to be angry. You have a right to be sad."

"I sense a 'Dr. Phil' lecture coming on." Delia wiped her lips with a napkin and set the hamburger back onto the plate. "What on earth are you talking about?"

"The drinking, dear. The risky behavior. Signs of depression, don't you think? And talking to someone—"

"Such as a *therapist?*"

"Well," Georgia said, hesitating a bit. "It wouldn't hurt. You've had quite a shock."

"Mom." Delia took a deep breath, exhaled and muttered something under her breath. Georgia didn't ask what she said. She picked up her fork and stabbed a chunk of chicken breast as if she and her daughter were having a casual Friday afternoon lunch and not talking about Delia's mental instability.

"I'm fine," Delia declared. "It hasn't been easy with the divorce and all, but I am *fine*. Really. I'm not the first woman in the world who's had her husband leave her for someone else. I don't spend my nights crying in my pillow."

"All right, dear. I just thought I'd make a little suggestion." She smiled brightly and shoved the chicken into her mouth. Georgia didn't believe a word of this "fine" business.

She was going to have to watch Delia like a hawk. Those nervous breakdowns were frightening events. Great-aunt Belle, on her mother's side, had locked herself in a room for six months once. Folks had whispered it was on account of "the change." Horatio, Belle's younger brother, said she had always been skittish. One day she came out of her room like nothing had ever happened and that was that, except for a slight facial tic.

"I think," Delia said, picking up a French fry with her fingers and then putting it back on her plate. "I think Uncle Gin's trailer is the answer to everything."

"What do you mean?" Georgia didn't think she was going to like the answer.

"I really want to get out of the house. All I'm doing

by staying there is making Martin's life easier. He can clean and pack the rest of the things by himself, or maybe he can get the kids to help."

"Them help? Those children of his haven't lifted a finger to do anything since the day they were born." Rude ingrates, all three of them. And the youngest, Jennifer, should be kissing Delia's feet for being a mother to her instead of walking around with her nose in the air acting like Delia was some kind of maid.

"We spoiled them," Delia said. "I should have been tougher."

"*Martin* should have been tougher." He'd let those three treat Delia like dirt under their feet.

"Well, I'm done with the place. I'm going to take my clothes and my beads and my books and move into Gin's."

"You can't possibly—" *Nervous breakdown*, Georgia thought. Her daughter was declining into a mental abyss of no return.

"Of course I can. I'm divorced, alone and free to do anything I want." Delia's smile was heartbreakingly brave.

"But people will think—"

"I don't care." Now the stubborn chin, the one physical trait she inherited from her father, lifted. Those hazel eyes held a warning: Mom, this is none of your business.

"Well," Georgia said, her chicken salad doing somersaults in her stomach. "I suppose I can say that you're out there at Gin's going through his things and cleaning the place up to rent out."

"I suppose you can say anything you want." Delia reached for her refilled glass of tea. "I'm looking forward to moving on."

"My home is always open to you, Delia," Georgia said, as she had so many times in the past months since Martin had turned into a lust-filled idiot. "When you get tired of that trailer and want your old room back."

"I'm not going backward, Mother." Delia picked up a pickle and took a bite. "I'm going forward. I've never lived alone, you know."

"Well," Georgia sniffed, remembering the odor of Horatio's mobile home. "It's vastly overrated."

"MRS. DRUMMOND, are you sure?"

"Of course." Delia smiled at the elderly woman behind the counter of St. Luke's thrift shop. "It's all yours."

"Oh, my, well, we can't thank you enough."

"It's my pleasure," Delia said, and couldn't have meant it more. She'd spent the last hour filling her car with boxes from her "Mrs. Drummond, mayor's wife" life and now those same boxes were stacked inside the basement entrance of July's only thrift store. "I hope you can make some money from these things."

"I'm sure we will, but—" The elderly woman gave Delia a sympathetic look. "This can't be an easy time for you, dear."

"You know," Delia replied, smiling. "This is the easiest part." And she meant it, long after she drove away from the thrift shop. The new Delia didn't need or want those fancy things any more—not the china or the crystal or the silver serving platters. Not the linen tablecloths or the polished silverware or the expensive Egyptian cotton king-size sheet sets. She'd left the first Mrs. Drummond's possessions packed in the attic—as they had been for thirteen years—for the children, who were old enough now to appreciate it. Maybe. And Delia would be damned if the next Mrs. Drummond—if Martin ever married Julie Brown, which Delia doubted—would use Delia's wedding presents for eating, drinking or sleeping.

No, she had been reasonable about this whole affair, divorce, losing the house situation, but she simply would not share wedding gifts as meekly as she'd shared her husband.

A woman, even a reasonable and perhaps dull woman such as herself, had to draw the line somewhere.

Delia pulled into the parking lot of the Wal-Mart on the edge of town and looked at the list she'd written after lunch, once she'd sent her mother on her way to her weekly card game and taken two more aspirin for her headache. Febreze, air freshener sprays, paper towels, Lysol and a small window air conditioner would be a good place to start. She'd pick up some instant tea mix, a plastic pitcher and some chocolate chip cookies, too.

That would be enough to get through the afternoon. She had her clothes, books and jewelry in the trunk, her makeup and shoes in bags on the floor of the passenger seat and her cell phone in her purse. She was ready to become self-sufficient and independent.

She was going to call her friends, get better at partying and, if she remembered the incident in her kitchen with J. C. Brown, she was going to have to improve when it came to flirting with men. She still blushed to think of how it must have seemed to poor J.C., whose reputation in high school had been that of a guy who could give orgasms with one touch of his fingers.

That skill had been discussed at several pajama parties, but since no one had experienced sex with J.C. the speculation remained just that. Maybe next time they were in a bar together she would ask him.

Or maybe not. She blushed thinking about it, which meant there was no way she was going to actually say such a thing out loud.

She was out of that man's league, always had been. It might be better to reactivate her single life with someone who was a little less skilled, a little less sexy. Wild and crazy sex was completely out of the question, but maybe having coffee or lunch with a man would be a better way to get back into dating shape. Then again, maybe men were more trouble than they were worth.

JOE COULD HAVE sworn he saw Delia stepping into the place across the road. He would have thought she'd be home taking aspirin all day, but then again, he didn't think the wealthy ex-Mrs. Drummond would be visiting anyone at the Pecan Hollow Trailer Park.

Not that it wasn't a decent place to live. Mostly retirees and a few young families starting out, but nice enough. And quiet, his mother assured him. He'd wanted to buy her a condo in Austin, but she wouldn't move away from July or from Julie and her kids.

Still, by the time he'd parked his truck in front of his mother's trailer and turned around to look again, the Delia look-alike had disappeared. He thought about calling the real Delia, just to ask how she was doing, but he decided against it. She might not remember much about yesterday and probably wouldn't want to be reminded.

He sat in his truck, rolled the window down and turned off the engine. He didn't know what the hell to do about his family. He'd come to July to rescue his mother and talk sense into his sister, but so far he hadn't accomplished much except buy a lot of groceries and pick up his mother's arthritis medication at the drugstore.

Last night's family reunion hadn't been anything to celebrate. Once he'd left Delia's white palace, he'd driven through the Burger Barn's drive-up window for a couple of hamburgers, then he'd gone out to see his mother. She'd been so thrilled to see him that he hadn't had the heart to tell her that he was in town to confront Julie. Mom assumed he was on vacation, didn't have a care in the world and had just stopped in to take her out to supper.

That had been the easy part of the day, even with his nephew Hank in a high chair and baby niece in one of those little carrier things on the seat beside him. The back booth of the Steak Pit had been a pretty wild place to be once Hank discovered that French fries were going to be part of his meal.

Then his mother had broken the news that Julie had gone off with her new boyfriend and wouldn't be back until Sunday. Meaning Joe was stuck in July for the weekend, when he'd planned to give the kids back to Julie today and take his mother back to Austin with him for a couple of weeks. She always liked visiting him and there were a couple of cousins of hers who were always happy to get together for dinner and an evening of the blues on Sixth Street.

His conversation with his sister—after she'd finally answered her cell phone—had been short and frustrating.

Joe grabbed the grocery sacks and climbed out of the truck. His mother's place was a double wide, one of the largest in the park. He'd put on a screened porch for her last year for her birthday when she wouldn't let him take her on one of those fancy cruises out of New Orleans. Betty Brown wasn't much for traveling.

He let the screen door slam behind him as he stepped inside the kitchen and looked at his mother, a baby on her hip and little Hank crying and clinging to her knees, and wondered how she could look so calm. But she looked exhausted, too, so Joe set the bags on the kitchen table before he reached for his nephew and swung the three-year-old into his arms.

"Hey, Hank, what's the matter?"

His nephew, blond hair sticking out all over his head as if he'd just gotten out of bed, frowned at him. "Nothin'."

"He wants his you-know-who," Hank's grand-mother said, sinking into a rocking chair moved from the living area to sit beside the kitchen table. There wasn't much room to walk around, but it was convenient for rocking baby Libby to sleep. "Been talk-ing of nothing else before and after his nap."

"Poor guy," he said over the boy's head. Hank wrapped his arms around his uncle's neck and rested his cheek against Joe's. The kid was growing fast. Joe could hardly believe how big he got since Christ-mas, when the family had come to Austin for the holidays. Julie had been ready to give birth any day and was more than happy to let her mother and brother entertain Hank, whose joy in life had been a set of plastic horses and a foot-high barn with doors that opened and closed. "I finally talked to her."

"And?"

He set Hank down. "Hey, buddy, why don't you get some of those little horses of yours and we'll go outside and build a ranch?"

"Like yours?"

"Yep. Just like mine."

"Okay." Hank hurried off around the corner and down the hall to the small bedroom he'd shared with his baby sister and mother since Julie lost her job.

"You go rest, Mom." Joe lifted the baby out of her arms and tucked her against his chest. "I can manage for a while."

"Tell me what Julie said first." She smoothed the baby's T-shirt over her plump tummy and Libby, pink and round and smiling, reached for her glasses. "No, sweetheart, Grandma needs those."

"She said she's not coming home until Sunday, like you said, but she's not sure about the future. I think she's having trouble talking her new boyfriend into playing Daddy to her two little kids." There'd been more, lots more, but Joe didn't share it with his mother. She hated to think her only daughter was a lousy mother with no conscience and very little self-control, but Joe figured his sister was also on some kind of pathetic search for love. And she wasn't real fussy about where she found it or what she had to do to keep it.

"That girl has a heck of a time with men," his mother said. "They can't resist her and she can't resist them and you know what happens next."

"Yeah." Babies. Like the one in his arms.

"You sure you're all right with Libby?"

"I can manage just fine," he lied. "When is she going to get hungry?"

"Not for a couple of hours, but she gets cranky in the afternoons sometimes." Betty smiled. "Like you used to."

"Go rest," he said. "I'll put the food away. And your medicine is on top of one of the bags."

"Thanks, honey." She went over to the table and rummaged through the plastic bags until she found the little bag that held her medication. "I kept meaning to get to town, but each day something would come up."

Like baby-sitting two little kids. And waiting for Julie to show up. A sixty-nine-year-old woman with arthritic knees and a lifetime of hard work etched in her face should damn well have the right to take it easy. He knew darn well she was trying not to limp, just so he wouldn't worry.

"You know I'm glad to help," he said, and the baby pulled on his ear and screeched. He went over to the sink and poured his mother a glass of water. When he handed it to her, she smiled again.

"You're a good boy, Joseph. Haven't I always said so?"

"Yeah. You always said I was your favorite," he teased, which made her laugh. She was still a pretty woman, plump and good-natured. She'd married a rodeo man with a loud laugh, a mean temper and an amazing ability to lose every job he ever got hired for. The years hadn't been kind, but somehow his mother kept a smile on her face.

"I'll just put the milk and eggs away." Before he could stop her, his mother had unloaded three of the six bags on the table and had found everything that needed to be refrigerated. He tried to help, but holding Libby was slowing him down.

"Who lives across the street?" He moved closer to the window. He didn't think he recognized the white Cadillac sedan, but it had Texas plates. There had been a similar white Cadillac in Delia's driveway yesterday, but he hadn't paid much attention to it. Still, the coincidence was unsettling.

"No one, not now," she answered. "Hank? Are you coming?" The boy yelled that he was "goin' potty," which seemed to make Betty very happy. "Good boy," she called. "You take your time and let me know if you need help in there."

"There's a car over there now and I saw a woman going inside."

Betty stood beside him to look, too. "Well, old Horatio died a couple of weeks ago. Maybe somebody bought the place. Or maybe that's his niece. Horatio was a sweet old man, but he didn't like company much."

"But he had a niece? Who would that be?" Joe had the sinking feeling he knew what she was going to say.

"Georgia Ball, the English teacher."

"The woman I saw was definitely not Mrs. Ball." The woman he'd seen *was* Delia, then, probably cleaning out her uncle's trailer. Made sense.

"If we have a new neighbor, I should go over and say hello." His mother went toward the door, but stopped. "Maybe I'd better put some brownies on a plate for her. It wouldn't be right to show up empty-handed."

"It wouldn't be right to show up at all, Mom." He

shifted Libby to his other arm and took his mother's elbow. Once she was seated in the rocking chair, he continued. "You know who Mrs. Ball's daughter is, don't you?"

Betty frowned and rubbed the tops of her thighs as if the muscles ached. "Who?"

"Martin Drummond's wife. *Ex*-wife. I don't think she's going to want a visit from us."

"Oh, dear."

Joe looked out the window again and saw Delia's cute little ass bent over the opened trunk of her car. *Would you like to have wild and crazy sex?* she had asked him. Yes, dammit, he would, but Delia had always been too good for him. Even yesterday, when she was drunk, divorced and looking for trouble, Delia had a smile that made him want to protect her from men like himself.

"We're going to mind our own business," he told his mother as she reached for Libby. "And we're staying away from that trailer."

4

"BEER OR BROWNIES?"

Delia was in the middle of lugging garbage bags out of the trailer's door when she saw J. C. Brown standing next to her car. A little boy stood beside him, his thumb stuck in his mouth as if he was uncertain about his whereabouts. Delia's first thought was that J. C. "call me Joe" Brown was even more handsome than she'd remembered from yesterday. And her second thought was that she should have guessed he was married. It was something she should have asked him yesterday, before she propositioned him. "What did you say?"

He smiled. "Would you prefer beer or brownies? I brought the beer and my mother baked the brownies," he said, indicating a plate wrapped in foil. "And she was determined to give them to you. She wanted me to tell you how sorry she was about your uncle."

"But how—"

"She lives across the street."

"Oh." Delia quickly tossed the bags, filled with kitchen rejects and old boxes of food, onto the dirt beside the metal stairs before making an effort to brush the hair off her face. "That's really nice of her."

"On the other hand," he said, holding up two dark bottles of beer between his fingers. "I know how much you like a drink in the afternoon. But to be safe, I only brought two. One for you and one for me."

"A woman makes one mistake and she's branded for life." She smiled at him, though, and held the door open. "Why don't the two of you come in and I can apologize again for yesterday."

The little boy's eyes grew wide and the thumb popped out of his mouth. He was a cute little guy, with all that hair sticking up on his head as if he'd never been tormented with a hairbrush. "Me, too?"

"Sure. What's your name?"

"Hank."

"Hi, Hank. I'm Delia."

"Hi." He gave her a shy smile.

"Hank is my nephew," Joe supplied, giving her a look that said he knew what she had been thinking. He followed Hank up the stairs, making sure the little boy didn't fall, while Delia backed into the living-dining-kitchen area of the trailer. "We're hanging out together while his baby sister and his grandma take a nap."

"Yup. Hangin' out." The boy nodded and Delia resisted the urge to smooth his hair. He was a stocky fair-haired child, unlike his lean uncle in looks and build, but the child clearly adored the man who entered the trailer behind him. He kept looking behind him to make sure his uncle was following.

"I'm cleaning," she said. "So you'll have to ignore the mess." She might have been a little hasty moving all her worldly possessions to Pecan Hollow. After opening all the windows in Uncle Gin's mobile home, the smell of onions permeated the place and let the heat in, a necessary evil considering the circumstances. "And it still smells like my uncle's cooking."

"It's *liddle!*" Hank peeked around the counter to the narrow hall that led to the bathroom and bedroom.

"It is, isn't it?" She tried not to laugh at the child's excitement. "It's the perfect place for one person."

"So, what are you doing here? Getting ready to rent it out?" Joe set the brownies on the freshly cleaned kitchen counter and popped open the beers. He handed one to her.

"Thanks. I'm cleaning it out," she said, taking a sip of ice-cold beer. "Because I've moved in."

"Moved in?" Joe frowned. "Why in he—heck would you want to live in this old place?"

"It suits me just fine." She looked around the kitchen and was glad she'd accomplished so much in such a short time. It had taken an hour to go through the small cabinets and toss most of the food into the garbage. The refrigerator didn't have much inside, but she had thrown everything out anyway and gave it a good cleaning. On her hands and knees, she'd scrubbed the vinyl flooring with a stiff brush and soapy water with bleach added. There was great satisfaction in knowing that she was the only one who would dirty it.

"It smells funny here," the little boy said, his nose wrinkling as he hopped up on a narrow brown couch.

"Yes, it does. My uncle cooked a lot of chili," she said, unwrapping the brownies, handing the child one of them. Delia had doused furniture cushions with the scented spray until she figured she'd done all she could. For now the place smelled like onions and flowers mixed together, which was a little strange, but nothing a person couldn't get used to.

"What do you say, Hank?" his uncle prompted.

"Thank you."

"You're very welcome." She turned back to Joe, who leaned against the counter as if he drank beer with her every afternoon. "So."

"So," he drawled, and they each took another swallow of beer. Delia broke the silence first.

"How did you know I was here?"

"I thought I recognized you when you were unloading your car. My mother knew that Horatio was related to your mother and she wanted to show her sympathy to your family. I guess he lived here a long time."

"I think he was the first one in Pecan Hollow."

"Tell me you're not moving into this, uh, place."

"Why shouldn't I?"

"It's not exactly your style." He looked around him at the brown built-in couches that lined two walls of the living area, at the windows now devoid of curtains—they were now in the garbage—and the battered paneled walls that were designed to look like wood, but weren't. "I've seen your white mansion, remember?"

"This suits me just fine," Delia insisted, though she had begun to have doubts about how quickly the place would be habitable. She'd yet to unpack any of the boxes of beading supplies stacked near the television. Once she'd cleaned the place, she intended to turn the living room into a workspace.

"Are you in some kind of trouble?"

"No." She gave him her sunniest smile and hoped she didn't look drunk again. "I'd rather be on my own than in Martin's house. And I have a lot of my uncle's things to sort through, so I thought it would be easier if I just did it here."

"In a hot tin can that, uh, smells like old food." He didn't look convinced, and he wiped his forehead on his sleeve, which reminded Delia that her body was damp with perspiration. "Is something wrong with the air conditioning or do you just like it this hot?"

"There's something wrong. Probably old age."

Joe leaned against the counter. "You want me to take a look at it?"

"No, that's okay. I bought a small air conditioner for the bedroom, so I should be fine for a few days until I can get a repairman to—"

"We're in the middle of a heat wave," he pointed out, setting his beer on the counter. "It'd be hard to take this kind of heat for too many days. Where's the unit?"

She pointed toward a tall utility closet near the door. "In there. Let me move the boxes—"

"Got it." He lifted the cartons that held Uncle Gin's music and moved them into the living area, next to an old wooden coffee table. She knew she shouldn't be gawking at the muscles in his arms, but she was only human. Delia hid a sigh and opened a drawer where she'd found a handful of screwdrivers and a measuring tape. She took all of the tools and set them on the counter, just in case they were needed, while Joe poked at the appliance that should have been pumping cold air throughout the trailer.

"The switch is off."

She walked over to see, which gave her a great view of Joe's back. "What switch?"

"This one." He clicked something near the bottom of the closet and a fan whirred to life and the machine hummed. "I guess someone must have turned it off. I didn't see any leaks from the valves or anything like that, but this thing is so old you might want to have someone come out and take a look at it anyway. If you plan to stay here."

"I will," she said, backing up. "Thanks."

"What about the one you bought?"

"I'm going to keep it, I think, just in case this one decides to stop working."

He shut the closet door and looked like a man who was pleased with himself and wanted to continue to do good deeds. "Where is it?"

"In my car, but—"

"I'll bring it in for you." He glanced toward Hank, who sat cross-legged on the couch while he ate pieces of a brownie in slow motion. "Stay here, Hank. I'll be right back."

"*No!*" The child looked terrified and the uneaten piece of brownie fell to the cushion as Hank scrambled to catch up with his uncle. "No, *no!*"

Joe lifted him up. "I'm going out to the car, buddy." He pointed out the screened door. "See that car? Delia has something heavy in there that has to come inside. Can you wait here and help open the door?"

Hank nodded and Delia put her hand on his tiny shoulder. "I'm really glad you came to see me today," she told him. "Don't worry. We can stand right here and watch your uncle, okay?"

He nodded, his thumb settling into his mouth while he looked out the door. Joe easily wrestled the box out of the back seat and carried it inside while Hank watched. The little boy's worried expression eased once his uncle was inside the trailer again. Delia had no experience with toddlers—Jennifer had been an independent five-year-old when Delia had become her stepmother—but the little boy's reaction seemed extreme.

"Bedroom?"

"Yes." She followed Joe down the hall and then the realization hit her. Of course. Hank's mother had to be Julie, the same woman rumored to be vacationing with Martin this weekend. She should have realized it right away, but then she wasn't thinking straight these days. She'd been too busy looking at Joe Brown's muscled body.

Poor Hank. She hoped he had a daddy who loved him, because unless Martin had changed completely these past months, he wouldn't have the patience for raising another family. He was relieved that she'd never become pregnant and he'd often said that he looked forward to Jen going off to college so he'd have a quiet house.

"You expected to hook this up yourself?" Joe dropped the box on the bed and turned around. "Tell me you're kidding."

"I was going to give it my best shot." She smiled. "And then I was going to hire someone."

"Good," he said. "At least you have *some* sense."

"I should be insulted," Delia laughed. "But lately I've learned that there's a whole lot of things I know nothing about."

"That's not your fault," Joe said, giving Hank a quick glance. The boy stood close to Delia, his head resting on her thigh as if he was about to fall asleep. She stroked his hair and he stuck his thumb in his mouth and closed his eyes.

"Yes, it is," she said, but she didn't feel like explaining. "Where's his m-o-t-h-e-r?" Delia watched Joe pull a jackknife from his pocket and slit open the tape that held the box flaps together.

"Good question." He didn't look up from his work. "I'd like the answer to that myself. She's taken off for a few days. To Vegas, maybe."

"Then she's who I think she is?"

"Yeah." Well, that was interesting. No wonder the

little boy didn't want his uncle to leave him a few minutes ago. Little Hank no doubt wondered where his mother was, too.

"So," Delia said, unable to mind her own business. "You live here in Pecan Hollow with your mother?"

"Hell, no." He turned to look at her and frowned. "I live in Austin."

"So you're just visiting." The little boy was leaning hard now, so Delia sat down on the edge of the bare mattress and pulled Hank up so that he was sitting beside her. In a few minutes she'd ease him down and let him sleep if he wanted. He seemed content as long as he could hear his uncle's voice.

"My mother sold the ranch a few years back and bought this place. She didn't want to leave July, though I can't figure out what makes her like it here so much."

"She's used to it, I imagine. The older we get, the more used to things we become." She'd become used to living with a polite stranger and thought that was the way marriage was supposed to be.

"My mother also won't leave because of the kids. My sister isn't the most dependable person on the planet and my mother picks up the slack by making sure her grandchildren are taken care of."

Delia had an opinion about a woman who wouldn't take care of her own little children, but she kept it to herself while Joe skillfully removed the air conditioner from its box.

"Which window do you want this in?"

It was a good question, because the bedroom took up the back of the trailer and had small windows on all three sides. Delia had removed the curtains and left the metal blinds.

"Wherever there's an outlet?"

"Good choice."

They both looked around the room, with Delia more aware with every passing second that J. C. Brown was in her bedroom. It shouldn't have been anything that would have made her self-conscious, except that he was so darned handsome and then there was that undeniably appealing "fix anything" aspect of the man.

Now that you've fixed my air conditioning and installed another unit in my bedroom, could you repair my battered ego and make love to me for a few hours as if I'm some hot babe you can't resist? Delia rolled her eyes. Those weren't the feelings a newly independent woman should be having.

"I can put it in there," he said. "No problem."

"Yes," she said, hoping she wasn't blushing as he pointed to a window above an outlet that had appeared after he'd moved a stack of books. "That would be fine."

"I left my beer in the kitchen." He grinned at her. "Are you one of those women who's going to yell if I ask her to get it for me?"

"No," she said. "I have no pride when it comes to cold air." When she returned with the two bottles, she handed him his and he smiled.

"I guess our afternoon happy hours are becoming a habit."

Delia grimaced. "Look, I'm really sorry about what happened yesterday. Thanks for, um, taking care of me."

"You're welcome."

"I really don't do things like that, like drinking too much and depending on a stranger to take me home."

"Yeah," he said. "I could tell." He picked up the installation booklet that came with the air conditioner. "You wouldn't by any chance have any tools around here, would you?"

"A few." She hurried to the kitchen to retrieve the screwdrivers. By the time she returned, Hank was asleep in her bed and Joe Brown, deep into Mr. Fix-It mode, had stopped talking.

Which was too bad, because Delia liked listening to him. She knew nothing about Joe, except that he was visiting his mother and he was handy with appliances. And he was sexy, whether a woman had had too many daiquiris or was completely sober.

Long after he'd taken Hank and left, Delia found herself staring across the road at the huge mobile home that belonged to Joe's mother. Green and white, with neat window boxes, a screened-in porch and a paved driveway, it looked like a palace compared to Horatio's old trailer. In fact, from what she'd seen, the other fifteen or twenty mobile homes looked nice. Uncle Gin's was clearly the eyesore, and the closest to the main road.

He'd told her once that Willie Nelson had bought it for him, after a song Willie had written hit the charts sometime in the seventies.

"Top of the line," he'd said, patting the couch cushions with great pride. "'Course I gave ol' Willie the chorus to that song. Dottie West wanted it bad, but we told her it was a man's song, and she threw a pot of beans at me. We laughed so hard I dang near hurt myself."

She would like to laugh that hard, Delia decided, looking at the old guitars hung on the wall above one of the couch sections. Maybe she'd turn out to be a hermit, too, Delia thought. Maybe it ran in the family.

Ignoring her plan to diet, she ate brownies and chocolate chip cookies for supper, and when it grew dark out she crawled into bed. The sheets were cool and clean, and the air conditioner's fan blocked out the noise of someone's party three spaces down, toward the Laundromat and the convenience store.

This hermit business was lonesome right now. Tomorrow she would go to a former neighbor's barbecue, the kind of party she'd been avoiding up until now. She would call Kelly, her oldest and still single friend, who wanted to spend Saturday night dancing at the Creek and was sure that all Delia needed was a night on the town.

Neither offer sounded particularly appealing, but spending another night alone in the trailer reading sheet music was too depressing to contemplate. Things would be better, once she figured out what she wanted to do with her life. If all else failed, she could learn to play the guitar and sing songs like another Uncle Gin classic, "A Hard Man is Easy to Find."

"Isn't there anything we can do?" Betty peered out the window Saturday morning and frowned. "She's still there. I can't imagine what that place looks like inside."

Joe could. While that trailer might have seemed like the height of luxury in the fifties, right now it looked like something that should be towed to the junkyard. "I don't think a woman like Delia Drummond is going to stay there for long, no matter what she says."

"She's lasted another day," his mother pointed out. "And she's piled up a lot of garbage. There must have been a ton of junk in Horatio's place. I'll bet that poor girl is going to be cleaning all summer long."

"I wouldn't worry about her, Mom." But he took his third cup of coffee and looked out the window, too. He couldn't help feeling responsible for her current trouble, but he'd done what he could with the air conditioning and he'd delivered the damn brownies. And when he was finished and had lifted Hank into his arms, Delia looked as if she was about to lose her one and only friend. He'd thought of kissing her, simply leaning over and taking a taste for himself, just because, well, just because she was so damn pretty and she'd looked so alone and maybe because he remembered her high school smile.

All good reasons to stay away from her.

"Go over and help her with those bags, Joe. She'll be all day lugging those to the Dumpsters."

"Mom—" He didn't mind having an excuse to look at Delia again, but he didn't want to act like a stalker, either. "Don't you think this is awkward? Julie took that woman's husband, for cripe's sake."

His mother wasn't going to leave it alone. "All the more reason to help her now. I'll fix her something nice for lunch. We'll have her over and I'll apologize for Julie's behavior."

"I don't think that's such a good idea."

"It never hurts to be neighborly, Joe." She started pulling food out of the refrigerator. "You think that Drummond fellow will return to his wife? Julie's never kept a man around for long."

"I don't know, Mom." The thought of Martin and Delia back together again didn't appeal to Joe at all, but he didn't stop to wonder why that scenario irritated him so much. Surely Delia was better off back in her white house on Lincoln Street than in Pecan Hollow, but that didn't mean she was so desperate that she'd take Drummond back into her life.

He turned back to the window and saw another black garbage bag fly out the door of Delia's trailer and hit the dirt. If she was a stranger, he'd be over there hauling trash, flirting, asking her out to dinner and hoping he'd get to spend the night.

THE NEWS quickly traveled around town: Delia Drummond, the former mayor's ex-wife, was forced to live in a rundown forty-year-old mobile home in the Pecan Hollow Trailer Park.

Such a pity, it was said. Martin Drummond should be ashamed of himself, him living in that new town house development on the south end of town. Luxury for the man, poverty for the woman. Some said Delia didn't have a dollar to her name; others said that life wasn't fair. Not to women, anyway.

Poor Delia, they said, shaking their heads when Lily May, chief owner and operator of Girls Curls, would have preferred they kept their heads still so she could get even cuts. Delia was sure having a hard time of it. Drinking, too. Acting wild, no doubt, and who could blame her?

Poor Delia, they said, drinking tea in the diner and looking for Georgia to arrive. Delia's mother would certainly have something to say about the situation. And why was Delia living out at Pecan Hollow when her mother had that big old place in town?

Poor Delia, they moaned, after word that she had been seen at the church thrift store a couple of days ago. Buying the things she needed, of course. Because everyone knew that Martin Drummond was spending all his money on his girlfriend. His *young* new girlfriend, the one who'd deserted her children and whose beauty was only skin deep.

"Delia's doing just fine, keeping busy with family things," was all Georgia said—to her card group, her friends at church and to Lily May when she got her hair done, as she did every Saturday.

"Women do strange things when their husbands leave 'em. That's the truth," Lily May agreed. "Next thing you know Delia will be piercing her body parts, and not just her tongue, either, if you know what I mean."

Georgia didn't even want to think about it. After she was washed, curled, dried and sprayed, she headed right over to Lincoln Street. She turned her back on the For Sale sign on Delia's front lawn and headed up Annie's driveway instead. There was no sense living in the past, as much as she preferred the days when her daughter was normal.

"We have to do something," she announced, when Annie opened the kitchen door. "I can't stand another day of this."

"I know, I know," Annie said. "Come on in. You want iced tea or a gin and tonic?"

"I'd better stick with tea, thanks." She sat in her friend's kitchen and rested her arms on the table. "What can I do?"

"I don't think you can do anything, Georgia. Delia's a grown woman with a mind of her own." Annie put the drink in front of her. "Your hair looks nice. You just get it done?"

"Yes. Lily May had quite a bit to say this morning."

"You shouldn't pay any attention to her. She's always sniffing around for gossip. You want a sandwich? I was just going to make lunch."

"I'm not sure I can eat."

"Sure you can. And then we'll buy Delia a nice

housewarming present and we'll go over and see that place for ourselves. Maybe it's not as bad as you think it is, now that she's been cleaning."

"It's bad, Annie. Real bad. You know how Horatio was. I'm surprised he didn't die of food poisoning. You wouldn't believe how bad that place smelled. I heard Delia's been to Wal-Mart three times for air fresheners."

"Well, that's good."

"Good?"

"Sure. It means she's making the place nice. Maybe it won't be as bad as you think."

"Oh, it will be, Annie. Trust me."

It turned out that Georgia was right, because as they drove into the trailer park development, she heard Annie gasp at the sight of Horatio's trailer.

"I told you so," Georgia said. "The rest of this place isn't bad, but this?" She gestured toward the rusted chrome-colored trailer. "This is beyond imagination."

And the people walking between bulging garbage bags to get to the trailer's door were an odd crew, too. A tall dark-haired man pushed a stroller and an older woman with gray-streaked blond hair held the hand of a little boy and carried a plate covered with tinfoil. Clearly Delia's neighbors were about to make a call.

"Looks like she has company," Annie said, when Georgia pulled the car onto the side of the road. There was no room in the drive, not with Horatio's old Buick and Delia's car. There wasn't going to be any room inside the trailer, either, not if the little family knocking at the door were invited in.

"I was hoping she'd have come to her senses by now." She turned off the engine and reached beside her for the plant Annie had insisted on bringing as a housewarming gift.

"It's so nice that her neighbors are—oh, my."

"What?" She'd forgotten to unbuckle her seat belt, damn it. She fussed with it until the latch opened, and then managed to get the strap away from her shoulder.

"Those are the *Browns*," Annie whispered. "Look."

Georgia looked, all right, the plant forgotten on the seat of the car. She had to squint a bit, but sure enough, she recognized a Brown when she saw one. Tall, lean, with dark hair and what some would call a handsome face, that was J. C. Brown, all right. And the woman was probably his mother, though that was just a guess on her part.

"I didn't know J.C. had kids." Annie stepped out of the car and smoothed her blouse over her slacks.

"I'll bet you fifty dollars that those aren't his. They have some nerve, parading that husband-stealing woman's children in front of my daughter."

"Oh, Georgia, Betty would never do anything like that."

"She's doing it, isn't she?" She started across the grass toward the trailer door when she saw J.C. knock on it. "You'd think they'd have the decency to leave her alone."

"Maybe they want to apologize," Annie whispered, hurrying to catch up. "They're carrying food."

"It'll take more than food to make Delia better," Georgia muttered. For the first time in her life she wished she carried a rifle. She could have pointed it at that herd of Browns and ordered them off her property. Betty Brown turned toward her and gave her a hesitant smile.

She should look nervous, Georgia thought. Because she'd protect her daughter from these people right down to her last breath. She opened her mouth to say so, but just then Delia opened the trailer door.

"Well, this is a surprise," she said.

No kidding. Georgia had to press her lips together to keep from screaming.

5

ANY THOUGHTS about being a hermit went right out
of Delia's head the minute she opened the door and
saw the people awkwardly gathering at the bottom
of the steps.

Joe, taking a chubby baby out of its stroller, was
the only one not staring at her with embarrassment
or shock. Even Annie looked a little nervous, though
she held out a flowering purple plant and said, "Congratulations on your new home!"

Georgia looked at Annie as if she'd lost her mind,
then turned back to Delia, who pushed open the door.
"Good morning, dear. We came to take you to lunch."

"This is a nice surprise," she said, trying to sound
as if the Balls and the Browns gathered together
every Saturday morning. "Thanks, Annie, that's really nice of you," she said, taking the plant. "Come
on in. Everybody, come in."

"Maybe this is a bad time," Joe said, after he managed to tuck the squirming baby against his chest.
She wore a pink sunsuit, a matching wide-brimmed
cotton hat and her little fists pounded her uncle's

white T-shirt. Delia sighed and resisted the urge to ask to hold her.

"No, it's a good time," Delia lied, wishing she wasn't dressed in bleach-stained shorts and a navy tank top. The plump woman next to Joe, holding Hank's hand, must be his mother, though they shared no resemblance. Joe's mother was short, plump and pale and she looked determined to say hello. Hank carried a foil-wrapped plate obviously meant as another gift of food. "It's fine. Really."

"Delia," Joe said, looking up at her with amusement. "I don't think you've met my mother, Betty Brown—"

"Hi, there, dear. We'll come back another day to visit," Joe's mother said. "We just wanted to bring you a little something to eat, that's all, Mrs. Drummond." She took the plate from Hank and handed it up to Delia. "It's nothing fancy, only fried chicken and potato salad. I'm sure you haven't had much time to cook, not with all the cleaning you've been doing."

"That's true, thank you. Please, call me Delia. Do you know my mother, Georgia Ball and her friend Annie Belmont?" Hank scurried up the steps and hurried past Delia to claim his spot on the couch.

It was Annie who sweetly said, "Oh, Betty and I go way back. But I'll bet it's been years since we've actually done more than smile and wave when we see each other in town. How are you, Betty? Do you still volunteer at the library?"

"Not for years," Joe's mother said. "It got to be too much for me."

"I have iced tea made," Delia offered, ignoring her mother's look of horror as she surveyed the pile of garbage bags in the yard. "Mom, are you coming in?"

"Is there *room*?" Georgia wasn't joking, but she was the first one up the steps. She clearly remembered what the inside of the trailer had looked like.

"Of course," Delia said, setting the plate and the plant on the counter as her guests filed into the living area. "I've been cleaning. Didn't you see all the garbage bags out there?"

"Well, yes," Georgia replied. "Are you sure you're ready to have company?"

"I bought paper cups and new ice cube trays yesterday." She could easily give everyone a cold drink and pass around the remaining brownies, though she'd eaten the last of the chocolate chip cookies for breakfast.

"I was real sorry to hear about Horatio," Joe's mother said to Georgia, who was busy sniffing the air like a hound dog looking for something to track. "He was a good neighbor. Quiet."

"My uncle kept to himself," Georgia said. "I guess that's how he liked it. It smells better in here today, Delia. Not so oniony."

"I've really been busy cleaning," Delia said.

"Horatio wasn't much for soap and water." Mrs. Brown nodded. "I bet he'd be glad to know that someone in his family is living here now and taking good care of his place."

"My daughter," Georgia said, "is *not* living here.

My daughter is going to come to her senses soon enough and move back to town."

Delia managed to thrust a drink into her mother's hand in hopes that it would distract her. Annie and Joe were discussing the baby, while Hank was sucking his thumb and watching the television, which wasn't turned on.

"Mrs. Brown?" She gave her a cup of iced tea. "Thank you for the brownies last night. I won't tell you how many I ate."

"Good for you," she declared. "You just can't go wrong with chocolate. Joe said he got your central air going?"

"Yes," Delia said, avoiding her mother's curious look. "He even installed an air conditioner in my bedroom."

"Your bedroom." Georgia's eyebrows rose. "How nice."

"Yes. I slept like a log." She filled two more cups with ice cubes and tea and moved sideways past her mother so she could bring Annie and Joe their drinks. Mrs. Brown seemed sweet. Whereas Georgia, peering into cupboards and opening drawers, seemed to be looking for something to criticize.

"Thanks." Joe took the drink. "Sorry we came at a bad time, but my mother can't stop worrying about you."

Annie sighed. "Delia's mother is the same way."

"Everyone can stop worrying," Delia said. "I'm enjoying myself. Hank, do you want a drink of water? I don't have anything else but tea, but when I go shopping today I'll get some lemonade."

"And choc'late milk?"

"Sure. I'll get that just for you, so whenever you come over you can have some."

"Okay." Hank gave her a quick smile and then snuggled against his uncle's side.

It was unfair that Joe looked so good holding that little girl. He shouldn't have, of course. He should have looked ill at ease and awkward as he sat on the couch with Hank's head on his shoulder and the baby in the crook of his arm while he listened to Annie brag about her grandchildren.

He could be married. Or divorced. He could have children somewhere whom he had walked and burped and fed and changed. And loved. And wherever he lived now, there had to be a woman. Or two. Or more. She didn't know anything about him, not really. His brother had been wild and had died doing some crazy stunt with a car, and his sister was wild in her own way, with two little kids and someone else's husband.

Those Browns, her mother had said years ago, are nothing but trouble. Well, to look at J. C. Brown now, anyone would think he was Father of the Year.

And as sexy as hell.

JOE COULDN'T get back to Delia for almost two hours, not with his mother's knee aching and Hank acting cranky and the baby upset because she was cutting a tooth. Julie was going to pay for this, he decided. When she came back to town his sister was going to take her own kids to a place of her own. He'd loan her money for an apartment and give her a long lecture about responsibility. She'd have to get herself together and start acting like a mother should act.

He wondered if such a thing was possible, considering Julie's track record. Mom had saved her from being out on the street more than once, had nursed Hank through chicken pox and Julie through her last pregnancy. There hadn't been any men standing in line to take credit for either one of the kids, and Joe didn't think her most recent conquest, Martin Drummond, was the type to be looking to take on two kids that weren't his own.

He hoped he was wrong, because those little kids deserved a better time of it than what they were getting.

Joe backed his truck across the dirt road to Delia's trailer and promised himself that he wouldn't knock on the door. He'd toss all those garbage bags into the back of the truck and haul them down to the Dumpster behind the Laundromat. That would be his good deed for the day. He would have liked to ask her out to dinner, but he didn't think there was any way she'd say yes. He wouldn't ask her out anyway, not even if he had the time, no sir. No longer a lovesick teenager, he was just helping out a neighbor.

Of course it was his bad luck that Delia opened the door right after he arrived. She was dressed for going out, in narrow black Capri pants that showed off her legs and a fitted white top with a wide neckline that plunged to a V between her ample breasts.

"Joe? What are you doing?"

"What's it look like?" He was aggravated that she was going out. Probably going somewhere to use that "wild and crazy sex in the pool" suggestion, only this time it would be an invitation to see her trailer.

"Like you're stealing my garbage."

He didn't laugh. Her breasts were round and full and high and he wanted nothing more than to drop the bag he held in each hand and head toward Delia, but he managed to turn away and concentrate on dropping the garbage into the truck bed. She wore pink lipstick and black sandals, and she probably had a date with some fine upstanding guy from town.

"Joe?"

"Yeah?" He didn't turn around.

"You're helping me too much."

"Yeah," he said, hearing her walk down the steps. "But you look like you could use it."

"I could have taken care of my own garbage. I'm not helpless."

He turned to look at her again. "You're going somewhere?"

"A barbecue."

He leaned against the side of the truck and allowed himself another sweeping examination of her outfit. "Must be a fancy barbecue. You look like you plan to drink four or five daiquiris and invite some guy home."

"That's not—" Delia hesitated. "There's nothing wrong with the way I'm dressed. And besides, I can take care of myself."

"Oh, really." She was about as innocent as a bunny in a snake pit.

"Sure."

"Do you think you could prance into the Cottonwood dressed like that and not have men coming on to you?"

"I'm going to a party at a friend's house, not a bar."

"Doesn't matter where you're going," he informed her. "You look like you want to get laid."

"I don't know what kind of barbecues *you* go to, but the ones I go to aren't orgies. And these are perfectly nice clothes."

"Don't go getting all huffy, Delia. When's the last time you had a date—and Drummond doesn't count."

Her chin lifted. "Fourteen years. Approximately."

"Times have changed, sweetheart. You sure you know what you're up against?"

"Thanks, Pa, but I've read the newspaper once in a while and I know about safe sex and date rape and carrying mace."

"You're carrying mace?"

"No. It's a potluck supper. I'm stopping at the grocery store for a fruit platter."

"Very funny." His gaze swept her face and lower,

to the enticing display of cleavage and satiny skin, before returning to her mouth. "You're looking for trouble, aren't you."

She smiled then. "I told you a few days ago that I need to get a life of my own. My husband told me I was boring, my mother wants me to move back into my childhood bedroom and all I want—" She stopped talking the second he ran his index finger along her jaw and tucked a strand of hair behind her ear. Her earlobe was soft and he let the pad of his thumb graze it, tickling the cluster of little gold bells that comprised one of her earrings.

"All you want is what?"

"Freedom."

"Freedom," he echoed, moving his hand lower, to cup the slender column of her neck. She stood perfectly still, those hazel eyes of hers staring up at him. Oh, he knew he should back away while he still could, but he didn't. Instead Joe bent his head and brushed his lips against hers in the lightest possible motion. "Freedom to do what? This?"

She didn't answer.

This time his hands framed her face. He meant to scare her, to make her think about what she was doing, but the plan backfired the instant he felt her lips soften under his. She was warm and sweet and to his surprise she didn't resist when he urged her lips apart. She tasted of lemons and sugar, and he wanted nothing more than to keep kissing her, to claim her mouth and feel the enticing heat of her tongue against his.

He turned her so her back was against his truck. Her hands moved to his waist and he gently leaned his body into hers. Her breasts were soft against him, her breathing ragged, her heart beating against his chest.

Joe knew he had to stop this before he swept her onto the ground or hauled her into the trailer or took her standing up against the truck. He forced himself to pull away from her, to lift his head and look down into a pair of stunned hazel eyes and lips that needed to be kissed for ten or twelve hours.

"I told you," he managed to choke out, though his voice was hoarse.

"Told me what?" Her hands dropped from his side.

"Told you that you couldn't take care of yourself. You're going to get in trouble, Delia, so be careful." He felt like the biggest fake in Texas.

Delia looked up at him, a smile on her lips. "Getting into trouble—" she hesitated, her eyes twinkling "—feels good."

"That's not what I—"

"Thank you," she said, giving him a friendly pat on the arm. "But I really *can* take care of myself."

Thank you? Joe stepped back and let her move away. She walked up to the steps and disappeared into the trailer. She didn't look back and she didn't say another word to him, so Joe returned to picking up the rest of the garbage bags and figured he'd just made another big mistake.

"I WAS LONELY FOR A WHILE" looked like one of Gin's most promising songs, though Delia wasn't sure she remembered how to read music. There were notations above some of the words. That was enough of an incentive for Delia to pull one of the freshly dusted guitars from the wall and try to remember where to put her fingers on the strings to make the chords sound right. She hadn't played the guitar since she was seventeen, after having taken lessons from Uncle Gin for four years. They'd spent more time playing gin rummy than playing the guitar, she remembered.

But she didn't have anything better to do, not with the barbecue over and Kelly having found the man of her dreams at the Creek bar before Delia called to tell her she'd meet her for a drink somewhere. She'd wished her old friend luck and driven home with a plastic container of leftover fruit salad Carol had urged her to take with her when she left.

So she'd picked up more groceries and returned to the trailer around ten-thirty, to think about Joe Brown's extraordinary kisses and her own reaction to passion. She thought she'd forgotten what passion felt like, but it had been heavenly to be reminded. Even if Joe was only proving a point, before kissing her he'd looked a little flustered by her outfit. It wasn't new. Last summer, when she'd still been married, her husband hadn't paid the least bit of attention to her cleavage. Martin had certainly never looked at her the way Joe had.

"I was lonely for a while, and I would have walked a mile, just to see your face," she sang. Not exactly poetry, she thought, but good enough for a few minutes' entertainment. She wondered why Uncle Gin never published any more of his songs. Had he tried and been rejected or had he been content to live in his trailer and sing to himself?

"I was misery you see, and it was for all to plainly see, that I wasn't in the race."

The lights were on across the road. Joe's truck was in the driveway, so he was home and not kissing any other women in July tonight. She kicked off her sandals, tucked her legs underneath her and leaned back against the cushions. This was definitely easier than being in a smoky dance hall.

"Oh, it hurts to be alone, and I never should have known, the pain you put me in." The pads of her fingers began to hurt, but she kept them pressed against the frets and strummed. *"Was it worth it, glad you asked—"*

She stopped to try to make out the rest of the line, then gave up and sang, *"Something, something, in the past, I was never meant to win."*

The outside lights went on, illuminating the Browns' driveway, at the same time Delia heard the wail of a police siren drawing near. She set the guitar aside and knelt at the window to see flashing lights turn in from the main road. The police car flew into the Browns driveway and a deputy jumped out. J.C. was being arrested? She couldn't imagine him doing anything illegal, not now, but then again, she didn't really know him all that well. Except she'd brought him home with her from a bar a few days ago.

Another siren wailed from the main road, but this time an ambulance turned into the trailer park and bounced to a stop in front of the Brown trailer. Delia leaped off the couch, slipped her feet into her sandals and headed for the door. *Not one of the children,* she prayed, hurrying down the steps. They were so little and anything could happen. She didn't stop running until she reached the opened kitchen door and saw the rescue workers leaning over someone. The sheriff's deputy stood next to Joe, who looked pale and worried. He looked over when she entered the crowded kitchen, relief crossing his face for a brief moment.

"Delia—"

"What's happened?" She stayed inside the door, unwilling to get in the way.

"We're going to take her to the hospital, J.C.," the paramedic said. "You want to ride with us?"

"I'll be right behind you." Joe hurried over to Delia and took her aside. "It's my mother. They think she's having a heart attack."

"I'll stay with the kids."

"I don't know how long I'll be gone."

"Don't worry about them. Go," she said.

He hesitated. "Libby should sleep through the night, but I think she has a bottle around five."

She had never given a baby a bottle in her life, but now wasn't the time to confess her inadequacies. "Okay. No problem."

"Thanks." He put his arm around her and hugged her to him for one brief moment, and then he was gone, behind the stretcher, the paramedics and the deputy. The sirens began again, before Delia could shut the door, but the sound soon became fainter. Several neighbors called to ask what was wrong, so Delia filled them in and wrote down their names and offers to help in any way they could. She turned off some of the lights and went into the living room. It was a large area, complete with navy-striped over-stuffed couches and an oak coffee table. The television was on, the volume low, and Hank stood in the hall. His little face was red and stained with tears.

"Hi, Hank," Delia whispered. "Would you like to come sit with me for a minute?"

He lifted his arms to be picked up. He was heavier than she thought he would be, but she snuggled him against her and sat down in a well-worn blue recliner. "Scary night?"

"Yes." His thumb popped into his mouth and he rested his head against her shoulder.

"Your grandmother wasn't feeling well," Delia said, wondering how much she should tell the little boy. "Uncle Joe decided she should go see a doctor. So I'm going to stay here and keep you company until he comes back, okay?"

Hank nodded and his body relaxed. They watched an old Western movie and after he fell asleep, Delia carried him down the hall. The first room held a queen-size bed covered with a feminine blue-flowered quilt. Across the hall was a smaller room, where a night-light illuminated the outline of a crib. A double bed, its covers rumpled and covered with stuffed animals and plastic horses, sat under a window. A nearby dresser held a changing pad, a stack of disposable diapers and an assortment of baby care products. Delia managed to tuck Hank into his bed without waking him or the sleeping baby.

She stood by Libby's crib for a few minutes, making sure the baby was breathing regularly. She touched the baby's delicate back and covered her chubby legs with the soft blanket. She would have loved to have had a child. Would Martin have left her if they'd had children together or would that have only made his betrayal so much worse?

She didn't miss him. She'd stopped loving him a long time ago. Her stepchildren had needed a mother and she'd done her best, even though they had never really accepted her or showed the kind of love she'd longed for.

It was better to be alone, Delia knew now. Better to be on her own and living her life the way she wanted to live it. Everyone had regrets—that was part of life—but she didn't need to spend any more time feeling sorry for herself and wishing for babies.

Or waiting for love.

HE WAITED all night to learn that his mother had had a mild heart attack. The nurses had been kind, the doctors brusque, the information brief but frightening. Her prognosis was good, but there were more tests to do, more to learn about her condition and what should be done. Joe drove back to Pecan Hollow at sunrise, after being assured that his mother was "resting comfortably." *Go home*, they'd said. *Get some rest. We'll call you right away if anything changes.*

He was wired from drinking too much coffee, weary from worrying and pacing and sitting in a waiting room waiting for news. The outside light was on, though the sun was almost up. And there was one light in the living room, though he couldn't see anyone through the windows. He shut the truck door quietly and made sure that when he stepped into the house he made as little noise as possible. He didn't expect to see Delia in the kitchen, holding Libby in her arms in the rocking chair.

"Hi," she whispered, concern evident in her eyes. "How is she?"

"Okay for now," he said, keeping his voice low. He stepped closer to look at the sleeping baby. She had milk on her chin and a little smile on her lips. "How's everything here?"

"Very quiet. Hank was a little scared, but he went back to sleep." Delia looked exhausted. He realized she hadn't slept while the children were in her care. There were dark shadows under her eyes and her skin was pale. The outfit he'd thought was too revealing was now wrinkled and spotted with baby formula, and her hair was a wild tangle of chestnut waves.

"You haven't slept, either," he said, wishing he

could take her in his arms and hold her. He sat down at the kitchen table instead. He saw that Delia had made coffee, but he was too tired to get himself any.

"I did," she said. "A little. I kept Hank company until he went to sleep." She kissed the top of the baby's head. "Tell me what the doctors said."

"She's 'stabilized.' That's the word they use, *stabilized*. It's her heart."

"I'm sorry."

"I think she's been keeping it from me," he said. "I thought she was taking all those pills for her arthritis. Her knees have been bothering her." He rubbed his aching neck. "I should have seen it coming."

"Why don't you get some rest?" Delia stood and put her hand on his shoulder. "I'll put the baby back to bed."

"Hank—"

"I'll stay while you sleep," she said. "In case he wakes up early."

It was an offer too good to refuse. It was odd that he'd never come home to anyone before. The women in his life had not lived with him, or even met his family. He'd kept those parts of his life separate. And now he wondered if he had made a mistake. It had been one hell of a night and here he was, coming home to Delia holding Libby.

He didn't like wanting things he couldn't have.

6

DELIA WISHED there was something comforting she could say, but the best thing Joe could do was get some sleep. It was an odd intimacy, holding a baby and telling this man to go to bed.

"I know you're right. And I will, in a minute." He leaned forward and touched the baby's hand. Her fingers curled over his index finger in a soft grip. "I've been calling my sister, leaving messages for her to get in touch with me right away."

"She hasn't called here." Funny how it didn't bother her to think of Martin and his girlfriend on vacation. She wondered what he'd think when he discovered that she'd left the house—and the last of the furniture—for him to deal with. He wouldn't be happy and he'd probably call to complain to her that she wasn't holding up her end of the bargain. It was a phrase she'd heard for years. Looking back, she wasn't proud of herself for putting up with it.

"She's supposed to be home today, but her saying that doesn't really mean anything. She hasn't called in days." He frowned. "How could someone go away and leave two little kids and not even check to see how they are?"

"I don't know," she replied. It wasn't as if Martin looked like Brad Pitt, or was so charming and rich that a woman would forget everything else and run away with him.

"I think they were in Las Vegas for a while. At least, that's what she told Mom."

"Martin always wanted to go there."

"Then why didn't he take you and go?"

She shrugged. "He used to talk about what his life would have been like if he hadn't gotten married so young. His first wife died and he married me to give his children a mother." The boys, eight at the time, had been cautiously polite, Jennifer bewildered and sweet. Delia had believed they would be one happy family.

"He told you that?"

"No, not that it would have mattered," she admitted. "I thought I was in love. I thought *he* was in love. It didn't turn out to be that way at all."

"He sounds like a real shit."

"He is." She smiled and Joe chuckled.

"Will he marry her?"

"I don't know." He was really asking if Martin would be a father to Julie's children, if he might stick around and give his sister a happy ending and the children a home. "I guess you'll have to ask your sister about that."

"None of her previous boyfriends have stuck

around to help raise the kids." The smile was gone and he eased Libby's fingers from his. "Want me to put her back to bed?"

"Sure. If you want to." She managed to transfer the baby to her uncle's arms, though she was awkward about it. Her fingers grazed his chest; her arms touched his hands, her heart jumped in a silly way. She pretended not to feel the shimmer of awareness that reminded her of yesterday's kiss. She tucked the pink blanket around the baby's legs and Libby kicked in protest.

"Don't you dare wake up now," Joe told the baby. "Your uncle doesn't have the energy to play."

Libby gurgled and waved her fists, but she yawned delicately and blinked at her uncle.

Delia smiled at both of them and decided that once again she was losing her mind. The whole thing was odd—caring for the children of the woman who ran off with her husband was one thing, but lusting after her brother was something else. She was just lonely, that was all. She'd get over it as soon as she adjusted to her new life. She'd get better at all of this.

"What's wrong?"

She looked up to see Joe studying her. "Nothing. Why?"

"You looked…never mind." He hesitated. "Why didn't you leave him?"

"I guess I should have," she replied. "But do you leave someone just because you aren't deliriously happy all the time? He cared about his family and he cared about me. At least I thought he did. The last few years weren't exactly filled with joy, but I never knew he was having an affair until December, when he told me he was in love with someone else. And had been for several months."

"I'm sorry." Joe stood and looked down at her. "And here you are taking care of Julie's kids. Not exactly fair."

"It wasn't fair of Martin to take your sister away from her kids, either," she pointed out. "Or to your mother."

"Yeah," he said. "That's why I came. I figured I'd talk sense into my idiot sister and give my mother a rest. From what happened last night, I'd guess I was too late."

"Maybe it would have happened anyway. At least you were here to call an ambulance."

"And you were here to watch the kids," Joe added. "Mom said to tell you she really appreciates it. She was so worried, especially about what Hank would think. He's not having the best time of it lately."

"Maybe she can talk to him on the phone today."

"Yeah. The doctor wanted her to rest and then they'd do more tests." He glanced toward the window. "Sun's up. I guess I'll get some rest after all. You sure you don't mind staying for another hour or two?"

"I'm sure." She would have been happy to hold that baby all morning, but she would never admit it.

He started to walk away, but stopped. "I'm sorry

about what happened yesterday, Delia. It was out of line."

"That's okay." She assumed that "what happened yesterday" meant that particularly toe-curling kiss, but she would never admit she'd been affected by it. Or that it meant anything. Not to a man with his experience. "You made your point."

"Yeah, but what you do and who you do it with is none of my business. I was being a jerk." Joe smiled, a little ruefully. "I can't say I didn't enjoy it, though."

"Go," she said, laughing a little. "Don't say another word."

After he left the room Delia stayed at the kitchen table and looked out the window. Her trailer was clearly visible, a light still on in the living room and her car in the driveway. She hadn't minded taking care of the children; she hadn't minded being useful. She actually *liked* being useful. Maybe her new life would include joining the Red Cross or working at a food bank or maybe she'd become the kind of lady who fed all the stray cats in the neighborhood.

But first, Delia decided, getting up to refill her coffee cup, she would ignore her fascination with Joe Brown and his wide chest, square shoulders and dark eyes that looked at her as if he'd like to take her to bed.

Julie Brown was welcome to Martin. In fact, she'd done Delia a favor. She'd never have met J. C. Brown again, wouldn't have had the satisfaction of cleaning Uncle Gin's trailer and setting up the first place she'd ever lived in on her own. She was thirty-three—it was high time she got her own life instead of stepping into anyone else's.

"HAVE YOU HEARD?"

Georgia yawned and looked at the clock on the nightstand, not that she could see the numbers without putting on her glasses. "Heard what, Annie? And what time is it?"

"After seven. You're not up?"

"I woke up at four and went back to sleep. What's going on?"

"Betty's in the hospital."

"Betty?" Still groggy, Georgia struggled to sit up. She'd been dreaming of being on a cruise and dancing the tango with three men who looked like Jack Nicholson, so she was relieved to have been awakened by the phone. She swore her feet were starting to hurt.

"Betty," Annie repeated. "Betty *Brown*."

Ah, *that* Betty. "Is she all right?"

"It was her heart," Annie explained. "I heard it from Bill Ripley when I got the paper—his aunt lives at Pecan Hollow because she lost all her money from gambling and had to move in with her cousin. The ambulance came and took her away."

"Annie, for heaven's sakes, is the poor woman dead or alive?"

"Alive, thank the good Lord, but—"

"That's good. But what?" She put on her slippers

and headed downstairs to make coffee. She could tell that Annie was wound up enough to talk all morning, even if it was Sunday and they usually went to church.

"Uh—"

"How old is Betty?"

"Just a couple of years older than me, but I thought she looked awfully pale yesterday, didn't you? And she had trouble getting up and down the stairs."

"She said she has arthritis," Georgia said, turning on the kitchen lights. She headed for the coffeepot, which she'd fixed last night so in the morning all she had to do was flick the switch to the On position. "But everyone our age has arthritis. The only strange thing about yesterday was that she brought Delia lunch and came inside to visit."

"Maybe she feels bad about what her daughter has done. It must be embarrassing."

"I suppose," she said, unwilling to believe that a Brown had any redeeming qualities. Georgia hadn't said much after leaving the trailer yesterday. She'd let Annie go on and on about how nice it was to see J. C. Brown all grown-up and taking care of his baby niece just like she was his and how clean old Horatio's trailer was and didn't the plant look good on the coffee table. Georgia had kept her mouth shut, seeing how she seemed to be the only person on the planet who thought the Brown family should leave Delia alone. She didn't want Delia all cozy and content in a run-down trailer park. She knew her daughter and she knew that the girl was having a hard time losing her husband, her house, her money and now her sanity.

"Georgia, are you still there?"

"Sorry. I was thinking about Delia."

"Did you talk to her about—?"

"No. It wasn't the right time."

"Oh." The way she said it made Georgia stop watching the coffee drip into the carafe as if she could will it to brew faster.

"Annie? What's going on?"

"Well, Bill's aunt told Bill that she called the house this morning to see how Betty was—I guess everyone was real upset about her being taken to the hospital, her being so nice and all, despite that daughter of hers and everyone thinks the kids are cute, but they don't know how Betty does it at her age, taking care of two little ones the way she does and—"

"Annie," Georgia interjected. "What are you trying to say?"

"Delia answered."

"Answered what?"

"The phone. Delia answered the phone when Bill's aunt called to ask about Betty. She must have been over there helping out with the kids."

Now she knew her daughter had lost her mind. It wasn't bad enough drinking in a bar with the brother and moving into a trailer park across the street from the mother, but now Delia was baby-sitting Julie Brown's kids?

It couldn't get any crazier. And the worst thing of all was that Georgia couldn't think of any way to stop the madness.

"JUST A MINUTE, please." Delia took the portable phone down the hall and stood outside the closed bathroom door. Joe was in the shower, but one of the doctors at the hospital wanted to talk to him. She knocked, but there was no response. "Joe?"

The water stopped. "Delia? Are you calling me?"

"A doctor's on the phone. He said to tell you that it's not an emergency." She heard the shower curtain being pushed aside and within seconds Joe opened the door and reached for the phone, which she handed to him.

"Thanks," he said, water dripping down his chest. A white bath towel was wrapped around his waist, but the rest of the man was naked. Gloriously naked. No wonder he'd had such a reputation in high school if he looked half as good back then. Lean, muscular, tanned and completely unself-conscious about wearing a towel, the man was pure male and totally dangerous.

She decided she liked dangerous men, not that she'd ever known any before now.

"That's good news," he said into the phone. He looked up at Delia and smiled. "When?" She took a step backward, but Joe reached for her hand to keep her there. "Sure. Tell her everything is fine and I'll be in to see her later on. And thanks again, Doc. I appreciate it." He set the phone on the edge of the sink and grinned. "She's going to be okay."

"Oh, I'm so glad." She gave his hand a little tug, but he didn't release it.

"Yeah. She's on medication and needs to take it easy, but she's okay."

"It's a good thing you were here."

"I was going to say the same thing about you." He tugged her closer and wrapped her in a hug. "Thanks. For everything."

"Uh, Joe—" She was going to point out that he was dripping wet and almost naked, but her hands touched terry cloth. She wasn't sure what to do with her arms—wrapping them around his waist was out of the question—and afraid that the towel would come unfastened and give her the kind of temptation she wasn't prepared to deal with.

He kissed her cheek. "Go home and get some rest, sweetheart."

She should have resisted him. She shouldn't have enjoyed the tickle of his breath against her ear or the way his lips grazed her skin. "Okay."

"Okay," he agreed, but he looked at her mouth when he said it. Instead of releasing her, he kissed her, a soft meeting of lips that lasted only seconds, a thank-you-for-your-help kind of kiss that really didn't mean anything.

"I—" she began, aware that she probably smelled like baby formula and looked like she'd slept in her clothes, which she had spent the last hour doing. The living room couch had been surprisingly comfortable and neither child had awakened and needed her since six o'clock.

But Joe kissed her again, and this time he kissed like he meant business. His large hands spread across her spine, holding her to him. His lips were firm and warm. She didn't stop to think about where to put her hands; they went naturally to his waist, to the cool damp skin above the towel, while she kissed him back.

How brave of me, she thought. How daring to return the kiss of a good-looking man wearing only a towel while two little chaperones slept in another room. He urged her lips apart; she felt an answering jolt between her legs, a swell of passion so unexpected it caught her breath. His tongue teased hers, his fingers lowered to the curve of her spine and splayed along her buttocks. She leaned into him, felt the arousal against her abdomen and marveled at his reaction. He was all heat and wanting and she was tingling and needy. It was the perfect kiss, except that they were standing up and one of them was fully clothed.

He backed her against the door frame before her knees gave out. "It's gotta be that blouse."

"What?" She looked at his freshly shaven chin and higher, to those lips that caused such amazing reactions to her body.

"That blouse." His gaze dropped to her cleavage. "It's—"

"A mess?"

"*Indecent* was the word I was thinking." He smiled, his gaze meeting hers. "We have a big problem."

She knew. She'd felt it against her, but "problem" was an interesting euphemism for a physical reaction. To be polite, she pretended innocence and asked, "What?"

"My towel is slipping." He shifted slightly, but his hands were between the door frame and Delia's rear.

"Wait. I'll—" She made an attempt to grab the towel but her efforts didn't work. The darn thing dropped straight to the floor.

"You want me," he said, but he was laughing.

"I think it's the other way around," Delia replied, feeling the heat in her face.

"Damn right," he growled.

"I'm not going to look down," she told him. "I'm going to turn around and walk back into the living room."

"And then what?"

"The next time I see you," she said, moving sideways as Joe released her. "You'll be dressed."

"And you? What will you be?"

"I'll be home," she said. If she stayed there was no telling what could happen, especially since there was this physical attraction thing happening. His face fell.

"Do you have to go?"

"Yes." She backed up into the living room and quickly turned around.

"Will you come back?"

"If you need me, sure," Delia answered, but she headed toward the kitchen door as fast as her legs could take her. She was tired, dirty and aroused, a strange combination. This had been gloriously fun, but Joe was responsible for two small children and a sick mother. She was trying to get her life together and start over again. It was no time for playing kissy-face with a Texas charmer.

THE PHONE didn't stop ringing. Joe answered it each time, hoping that Julie would be on the other end, but the callers were his mother's neighbors inquiring after her health and offering their help. They knocked on the door, too. One woman brought a pie, another a macaroni and cheese casserole. A plump white-haired man delivered a bouquet of daisies in a canning jar while Hank cried for chocolate milk on his Cheerios. Joe thanked everyone and tried to remember their names; his mother would want to know.

"Deeyah's got my mulk," he said, looking at his uncle as if Joe was responsible for Delia's non-appearance at the kitchen table.

"How do you know that?"

"She said."

"Okay." He glanced across the street and wondered if she was sleeping. He had no idea if she had a phone over there, but as soon as Libby woke up they could go over and see if she was awake. Chocolate milk was as good an excuse as any, he supposed. Even if he had no business lusting after a freshly divorced innocent like Delia. She would be easy prey for some guy with an understanding smile and a sympathetic ear. Especially if she continued to run around town by herself, looking for fun and guzzling frozen rum drinks.

He hated to see anything happen to her. She wasn't the type who could wake up next to a stranger in the morning and not feel ashamed of herself. She might very well fall for the first guy who smiled at her, the first s.o.b. who told her she was beautiful.

Well, she was beautiful. That was no lie. Those hazel eyes and golden brown hair and lips that could make a man weak in the knees and hard between his legs. She had breasts—real breasts—that would fill his hand and then some. She was all female, curvy and soft the way a woman should be. He'd never been much for bony women, though he usually liked his women tall.

But Delia was sized just right.

But his sister's behavior had reduced her to near poverty. She had to sell her home and move into a trailer that smelled like chili and fried vegetables.

"Uncle Joe." Hank tugged on his shirtsleeve. "Where's Gramma?"

"I told you, Hank, remember? She's in the hospital having a little rest."

The boy nodded. "Her heart hurts."

"Yeah, her heart hurts, that's right." He ruffled the boy's hair. Hank didn't look anything like a Brown and only faintly like his light-haired mother, but Julia had informed the family that she didn't know who Hank's father was, so they could all quit asking her about it. When she was pregnant with Libby, the baby's father was some truck driver who drove off into the sunset the minute he heard that he'd given Julie, waitressing at the truck stop on Route 79, more than a big tip and a couple of months of sweet talk.

God, he hoped Martin Drummond was smarter, because Julie sure as hell wasn't. She'd been a decent little kid, a little wild but that streak ran in the family. Maybe it was time he had a talk with Martin Drummond, Ass Extraordinaire, about just what the hell was going on.

Joe looked toward Delia's trailer again. He'd like nothing better than to walk over there and make love to her. It was all he could do this morning not to unbutton that blouse and scoop those soft breasts into his palms. She wouldn't have stopped him, either, not the way she was kissing him. He'd had a crush on Delia when he was sixteen and repeating algebra class. Now here she was again, only now he wasn't "Bad Ass Brown" and she was no longer "Saint Delia."

He was thirty-five years old. He had a decent job, a nice little ranch he was fixing up north of Austin, and a nagging sense that there was something missing in his life. A wife? Maybe. But he'd never met a woman he could picture living with for the rest of their lives.

Until now.

When the woman of his teenage dreams was living in the same trailer park.

7

DELIA COULDN'T SLEEP. Not after kissing a near-naked Joe. Even though she crawled into her bed, closed her eyes, drew the curtains against the morning sun and willed herself to get some rest, she couldn't stop remembering how he felt against her. A man had no right to taste that good or kiss so well that the idea of having sex on the bathroom floor had actually held a great deal of appeal.

So she took a shower, put on fresh clothes, brewed iced tea and watched the Sunday morning news shows on Horatio's small television. She also paced around the small kitchen trying not to look across the street at the Browns' windows. No doubt Joe was busy with the children, something that was still difficult for her to relate to the wild young man she'd known in high school.

He was still wild, though. Wild enough to kiss her like he wanted to haul her off to bed, crazy enough to laugh when the towel came unwrapped and left him naked.

He'd smelled wonderful. Droplets of water from

Play the Lucky Hearts Game

and get...

2 FREE BOOKS
and a FREE MYSTERY GIFT...

yes! YOURS to KEEP!

I have scratched off the silver card. Please send me my **2 FREE BOOKS** and **FREE mystery GIFT**. I understand that I am under no obligation to purchase any books as explained on the back of this card.

Scratch Here!

then look below to see what your cards get you... 2 Free Books & a Free Mystery Gift!

342 HDL D343   142 HDL D35M

FIRST NAME

LAST NAME

ADDRESS

APT.#

CITY

STATE/PROV.

ZIP/POSTAL CODE

(H-T-10/04)

Twenty-one gets you
2 FREE BOOKS
and a **FREE MYSTERY GIFT!**

Twenty gets you
2 FREE BOOKS!

Nineteen gets you
1 FREE BOOK!

TRY AGAIN!

The Harlequin Reader Service® — Here's how it works:

his hair had tickled her ear and his skin had been warm and damp. He'd wanted her, which was something. She wondered if he regretted turning down last week's tipsy suggestion that they make love in her swimming pool. She'd thought she'd been very daring, but maybe she'd only been desperate instead. Desperate to be wild, desperate to be loved.

What an embarrassing afternoon that had turned out to be.

She really needed to have sex. That was obvious. But with Joe? No, he wasn't for beginners. And despite thirteen years of marriage, she felt less than experienced. No doubt he'd had lots of women. He probably knew more positions than the average male. She'd experienced what he could do with his tongue—just his tongue—for heaven's sake. Imagining what he could do with the rest of that lean, hard body almost sent her back into the shower.

No, she thought, plopping ice cubes into a tall glass. Sex with J. C. Brown was something that scared the heck out of her, a not-so-thin suburban stepmother, a divorcée who hadn't been made love to for longer than she could remember. Last fall she'd thought Martin's lack of interest in the bedroom was because she wasn't sexy enough or that he was having a midlife crisis. It had never occurred to her that he was having an affair, not even when her own friends questioned Martin's golf weekends and long nights at the office.

How stupid she'd been. Or maybe she hadn't

wanted to see what was going on. She'd cooked and
shopped and cleaned, but she'd been happiest alone
in her sewing room stitching beads onto crazy quilts
and attempting to replicate Victorian beadwork. She
hadn't exactly put a lot of time into wondering what
was wrong with Martin.

Delia sat down on the couch, her back to the street
and temptation to think about Joe, and made a list of
what she would buy for the trailer—new curtains,
throw pillows, a bright rug—and studied the living
room to see how she would set up her beadwork. She
had lots to do. There was an unfilled order for beaded
flowers, Uncle Gin's songs to put in notebooks and,
if she was really desperate for distraction, she could
call her mother and meet her in town for Sunday
dinner.

Or not.

She pulled the carton of songs close to the couch
and added "page protectors" to her list. If she was
going to organize Uncle Gin's music she might as
well do it properly. It was the least she could do for
the man who had given her a place to live. And besides, his songs deserved to be saved. Maybe someday she'd learn to play his guitar and go out on the
road singing "I'll Be Dead And Gone Before I Miss
You" and "Old Men Need Lovin', Too."

She was in the middle of learning the chords to
"Lay, Granny, Lay" when a familiar knock inter-
rupted a song she suspected was a satire of an old
Dylan tune.

"Come in!" Delia set the guitar aside as Hank opened the door, his uncle close behind him. Joe wore jeans and a University of Texas T-shirt, cowboy boots and an air of domesticity that was oddly touching. Libby, in a blue sunsuit and matching lace-trimmed hat, was in his arms. Her chubby feet were bare and her little hands kept trying to grab her uncle's chin. Delia steeled her heart.

Joe gave her one of his charming smiles and shut the door behind him. "As you can see, I brought the chaperones," he said. His gaze ran over her body and he sighed.

Hank tugged on her hand. "Dee-yah?"

"Hey, Hank. Did you come for your milk?" She couldn't help smiling at the child. He looked so serious, despite the ever-present cowlick and the wide blue eyes.

Hank nodded. "Yes, please."

"I didn't know you played," Joe said, looking at the guitar before meeting her gaze.

"I don't." She refused to blush when he looked at her as if he would like to take her into the bedroom. She wondered if he really meant it or was that simply a look he wore all the time.

"And the guitar?"

"It belonged to my uncle. I'm learning some chords so I can play his songs." She untangled her legs and stood, ruffling Hank's hair as she passed him on the way to the refrigerator.

"Hank was pretty insistent that we come over here."

"I'm glad he remembered. I should have brought it over to him." She took out the carton of milk. "Do you want to drink some here or take it to your house?"

"My house?" The child looked at his uncle.

"Grandma's house," Joe explained and Hank grinned.

"Okay."

She handed him the unopened carton. "There you go, pal. It's all yours."

"What do you say, Hank?"

"Thank you." His eyes were huge as he cradled the quart of milk.

"You're very welcome. You might not want to drink it all at once, though."

"Why?"

"Because you might get a sick tummy." Libby smiled at Delia and tipped toward her, her pudgy arms reaching down to be held. Delia laughed and took her.

"Thanks," Joe said.

"I promised him," she said.

"That's not what I meant." He glanced toward Hank, whose attention had been claimed by the guitar lying on the couch. The child patted the strings with gentle fingers and broke out into a huge smile. "I keep forgetting how awkward this is for you, being with Julie's kids and all."

"My mother has already left three messages on my phone telling me to stop being a fool."

He smiled, that slow sexy smile that made her heart race. "I don't think that's what I'd call you."

"No?" She smiled at him, flirting shamelessly, heaven help her.

"Absolutely not." He ran one roughened finger along her jaw and stopped at her chin. He looked as if he wanted to kiss her again, but she didn't think that would be a good idea in front of Hank. He might tell his grandmother or worse, his mother, and then it would be all over town. *Delia Drummond was seen kissing with J. C. Brown and you all know what that leads to.*

"You're very…kind."

"Kind?" She expected something more flattering, like *sexy* or *gorgeous*, things she aspired to. Of course, after eating cookies and brownies for two days, she should be relieved that Joe didn't say "maternal" to describe her since she could have put on another five pounds.

"And lonely," he added, looking at her mouth.

"Which makes me sound very pathetic," Delia said, stepping away from his touch. "Like an old auntie or some old lady who takes in stray cats."

"I didn't mean—"

"It's okay." She returned the baby to him. "I'll have you know I'm not lonely. I even have a date tonight," she lied.

"You do?" Libby started to fuss. He tucked her against his shoulder and patted her back, but the baby only screamed louder. "With whom?" Delia ignored the question, mostly because she couldn't think of anyone she'd care to spend an evening with. "I'm not trying to pry," he said, but he didn't look happy. "But you have to be careful. Men think recently divorced women are fair game."

"I've caught on," she said, remembering Martin's partner's advances last week. "And I think I can handle it."

"You *think*."

"I'm not a kid," Delia pointed out. But if the baby hadn't been in Joe's arms, she might have stood on her toes and kissed the frown off his mouth. He had a beautiful mouth and a chin with the tiniest indentation. It was great fun to flirt with him, whether he thought she was fair game or not. And even more fun to be kissed by him. Nothing serious, of course, but great for a very squashed female ego.

"No," he said, those green eyes unreadable. "You're not."

It was time to change the subject, so Delia took a deep breath before she asked, "How's your mother doing?"

"That's another reason why I came over," Joe admitted. "I was going to ask if you'd watch the kids while I went to the hospital this afternoon. There've been a lot of offers from the neighbors, but no one's under sixty-five." He smiled. "I think you're the only one in Pecan Hollow who could survive a couple of hours with a baby and a busy three-year-old."

"Of course I'll help. What time?"

"You'd really do that?" He winced as Libby hit a piercing high note.

She laughed. "That's what kind and lonely people do."

"You're not going to forgive me for that one, are you."

"Your niece is hungry."

"She's always hungry. Look, Delia, I don't think you're pathetic." He looked around the room, at the clean kitchen, the unpacked boxes, the brown sofa cushions. "But you have to admit, this is a long way from that big house in town."

"Thank goodness." He didn't look as if he believed her.

"Libby, darlin'," he crooned, easing the baby's temper as he rubbed her back.

"What time?" she asked again. "I'm going to town now, but I'll be back in an hour."

"Visiting hours start at one o'clock."

"Okay. Bring the kids over then."

"Here?"

"I'd rather not be at the house in case your sister comes back from Las Vegas."

"Yeah," he said. "I can understand that."

"Dee-yah?" Hank carried the guitar to her. "What is it?"

"A guitar," she told him. "You're going to come visit me after lunch and I'll show you how to play it."

"'Kay." Hank handed it to her and retrieved his

quart of milk from the small kitchen table. "Uncle Joe? Libby's hungry."

"Yeah. I know." He didn't look as if he wanted to leave, but he turned toward the door. "Come on, Hank. Let's go drink that chocolate milk and play with your horses."

"Bye." Delia held the guitar by the neck and watched the little family leave the trailer.

Joe helped Hank down the narrow stairs before turning to look back at her. "The real pathetic Drummond is Martin, you know. Not you."

"I know."

"Yeah." He winked at her. "But if you do get lonely, come on over."

She decided that didn't deserve an answer. With her free hand she waved at Hank and then shut the door. It was going to be a busy day after all—Wal-Mart, babysitting and a date. All she had to do was come up with a man for tonight.

At least a date would take her mind off getting naked with J. C. Brown. Lonely and pathetic? Sure. But she didn't have to advertise it by getting drunk by herself on strawberry daiquiris again. She could hear the town now: *Delia Drummond, that nice girl, has gone plumb crazy since her husband left her. Kissin' all sorts of men, raisin' a ruckus. And she used to be so nice, too. Wonder what happened?*

J. C. Brown kissed her, that's what.

"Promise me, Joseph."

"Mom—" The look on his mother's face stopped

his protest. How was he supposed to argue with a woman in a hospital bed? And she'd called him "Joseph," another sign that she meant business.

"You're not to tell her. Between the two of us we can manage just fine."

"The two of us," he muttered. "A man who's never had kids and a woman with a bad heart. Oh, yeah, we can handle Libby and Hank, no problem. No reason to call their mother."

"We can," she insisted. Sarcasm was wasted on Betty Brown. "They're good children."

"That's not the point. They're *Julie's* children and she should be the one taking responsibility for them." He sounded like a damn prig, even to his own ears. But damn it, he'd come home to talk sense into his sister and he didn't want to be deprived of the pleasure.

"She does her best," his mother said, which was a response he'd heard before.

"It's not good enough and you know it."

Betty sighed and looked toward the window. "It's too nice a day to be in the hospital."

"You'll be out in a day or two," he assured her, repeating what the doctor had told him. "As long as you take your medication and get plenty of rest, you'll do just fine."

"I know." She turned her head to smile at him. "If Julie calls, you're not to tell her I'm in the hospital, remember."

"I've left messages on her cell phone telling her

to call me. Not that it's done any good. I've been telling her to get her ass back here and take care of her children."

"Julie's got…problems," his mother said. As if that was news. "I think this Martin fellow will be good for her. He was mayor for almost nine years, you know. That shows he has a good head on his shoulders."

Joe slumped in the vinyl guest chair, his booted feet stretched out in front of him. Drummond might have a good head on his shoulders, but that wasn't the part of his body that was making decisions for him lately. How the man—mayor or not—could walk out on a sweet, sexy lady like Delia, well, Joe couldn't figure that out.

"Maybe," his mother continued, "he'll be a good influence on Julie. Settle her down."

"He cheated on his wife. You call that being a good influence?"

Betty smoothed the blanket covering her and fidgeted with controls that made the head of the bed move. "Don't be so belligerent, Joseph. People make mistakes. That's just the way life is."

"Mistakes," he muttered, remembering a father who, when sober, had been one hell of a nice guy but whose downfall was the booze that eventually killed him. And then there was Jack, dead at eighteen when his mistake was to fight with his girlfriend, drink a couple of six-packs at a picnic and then drive too fast on the way home. "It seems we've had our share of mistakes in this family."

"But not you, Joe. Look what you've done with your life." She reached for his hand and he leaned forward to take it. "I'm real proud."

"I'm not going to let Julie mess up her kids," he warned. "I'll take them myself before I'll let her hurt them."

"She's a good mother," Betty insisted, twisting the thin cotton blanket between her fingers.

"When she's around, maybe," Joe said. "Like Dad was a good father—when he was around?" His mother grimaced and Joe immediately felt guilty for upsetting her. He squeezed her hand. "Don't worry. I wouldn't hurt Julie for anything, and if she shows up happy to start taking care of her kids, I'll wish her well and go back home."

Right after he kissed the Tooth Fairy, wrote to Santa and hopped around the yard with the Easter Bunny.

"Don't look so grouchy, Joseph." His mother squeezed his hand and smiled. "At least you have that nice Delia Drummond to keep you company."

"Yeah," he managed to reply. That "nice Delia Drummond," the woman who had just about brought him to his knees this morning with one long, sweet kiss, was an irresistible distraction in an already complicated situation.

A couple of weeks ago his life had been relatively simple. Summer vacation, plans to add on to the barn, giving his mother a few fun days in Austin.

Now here he was in July, his sister's latest escapade keeping him here for God knows how long. He sure didn't mind helping his mother or hanging out with the kids, but Delia? She wasn't his kind of woman, no way.

Which of course was the biggest lie he'd told himself all year.

"COME ON IN," Delia whispered, opening the door to admit Joe. He looked tired, but his visit with his mother must have gone well because the worried expression in his eyes was gone. "But keep your voice down. Libby just went to sleep."

"Thanks." He took three strides into the living room and sat down on the couch. Hank, busy with his plastic cowboys and horses on the floor, didn't bother to look up until Joe bent down and touched his shoulder. The boy smiled and climbed up on the couch beside him, snuggling against his side as Joe put his arm around him. "Grandma's coming home tomorrow, if everything goes okay. She has new medication and orders to take it easy." He leaned back and rested his head against the back cushions.

"Okay," Hank said, popping his thumb in his mouth.

"You can put your feet on the coffee table." She sat down across from him in the old recliner.

"Yeah?" He looked at the scratched old table as if he was afraid to hurt it.

"Go for it," she said, and watched as he made himself comfortable, boots crossed at the ankle resting on the scarred wood surface. "Do you want me to call my stepdaughter? She'd know how to reach her father. She's been staying at the condo with him until she leaves for college."

"What condo?"

"He bought a place on the other side of town. Hidden Valley Acres."

"Yeah." Joe grimaced. "I saw it on my way in. It's not hidden and there's no valley."

"No." She laughed. "It looks hideous, but Martin likes new things."

"And you? What do you like?"

"Old houses with porches. And furniture that isn't white."

"What else?" He closed his eyes as if he was enjoying the sound of her voice.

"Big dogs. The bead shop in San Marcos. Jelly doughnuts. Guacamole dip." *Green-eyed men wearing jeans and cowboy boots. Kisses at dawn.*

"I don't suppose I can take you back to Austin with me."

She shook her head. "I like my trailer."

"Too bad. I have a porch *and* a dog," he murmured, his eyes still closed. "You'd have to bring your own jelly doughnuts."

"Doughnuts?" Hank looked up at his uncle. "I like doughnuts, too."

"I'll get some this week," Delia told the child. "Just for you."

Joe sighed and opened his eyes. "I'd better take the kids home. Come over later and I'll fry up some steaks." He set his booted feet on the floor and lifted Hank off the couch.

"I don't think that's such a good idea."

"You don't like steak?" His eyes narrowed. "I know damn well you don't have a date tonight. You're a terrible liar."

"What do you want, Joe?" She stood and looked up at him. "What are you doing?"

He threw up his hands in surrender. "I offered you a meal, sweetheart. And I've got a bunch of food from the neighbors to eat. But I don't blame you if you want a break from us."

"That's not it and you know it."

"Do I want to sleep with you, is that what you're asking?"

She nodded.

"Well, of course. Who wouldn't? But I don't do one-nighters anymore. Too old." He grinned and put his hands on her shoulders. "You're alone and so am I. Come over at seven."

"Okay," she heard herself say, though she knew better. With her luck, Joe would end up taking care of his sister's children for the next eighteen years and she—softhearted fool that she was—would end up helping him.

Been there, done that.

Treating him as an overnight sex object was another option, but she still thought that was setting herself up for certain disaster. Even if it was tempting to see what it would be like, J. C. Brown was way out of her league.

8

OF COURSE HE'D lied about wanting to spend the night with Delia. And he was a hell of a good liar, too. Growing up with a drunk for a father could do that to a guy. Self-protection was the name of the game, though Joe didn't like remembering those years.

Joe knew damn well he'd settle for one night with Delia. At *least* one night. He was too old to wake up with a stranger in his bed, true. But the thought of eight or nine hours spent making love to Delia was beginning to haunt him. That lush little body would take days—and nights—to explore and even then he sensed that he still wouldn't be satisfied. He'd reactivated a high school crush and he was mooning around like he was seventeen again and Delia had smiled at him in the school corridor.

How pathetic was *that?* And how unsettling to wonder if the woman would let him kiss her again.

She was late for dinner by at least fifteen minutes. He seasoned a couple of thick steaks, set the table, fixed drinks, checked in with his mother and opened a beer. Libby wouldn't stop crying, Hank had asked for his mommy three times in the past hour and Joe's dream of an intimate, quiet dinner with his neighbor evaporated every time one of the children needed his attention.

Hank had given up and fallen asleep watching television, but the baby wasn't so easily distracted. Libby continued to wail against his shoulder, but he didn't know what else to do. He'd managed to change her diaper, he'd fed her, burped her and walked her from the kitchen to the living room more times than he could count. He almost missed hearing the knock on the door, thanks to his niece lifting her head to scream in his ear. When he opened it, Delia looked from him to the baby and raised her arms—not to embrace the man who stood staring at her as if he'd never seen anyone so beautiful, but to take the sobbing child.

"Hi," she said, looking up at him again with that sweet smile that made his groin ache. "How's Uncle Joe doing?"

"Not too well. Until now."

"You look very domestic." And she looked as if she was trying not to laugh. "What's the matter?"

"I've fed her, changed her diaper—and for that I deserve a medal—and burped her. But she won't stop—" Libby snuggled into Delia's neck and hiccupped. "Crying," he finished, backing up to let Delia enter the room.

"There, Libby, it's okay." Delia patted the infant's back.

"It's because I don't have breasts, isn't it?"

She laughed, a sound that made him want to make jokes all night. "That could be your problem," Delia said, walking over to the counter to look at the steaks waiting to be grilled. "You weren't kidding about dinner."

"A man's gotta have meat. These," he announced, "are from my very own cattle."

"You're a rancher?"

"Part-time." He picked up the platter. "I'll be right back. I'm going to put these on the grill and then I'll fix you a drink. Hank's asleep in front of the television and if you can keep Libby from screaming again I'd be grateful."

"Okay."

He tossed the steaks on the grill, checked his watch and hurried back inside where Delia waited for him. She was in the rocking chair, the baby tucked in her lap and, except for the television, the house was quiet. He had the inexplicable urge to stop and hang on to the moment, because it seemed so damned right. And he'd always wondered what it would be like to be part of a normal family, to care for his own wife and children and to make sure they were safe and happy.

"What's the matter?" Her voice was low, her gaze quizzical.

"Nothing." He cleared his throat. "What can I get you to drink?"

"Beer is fine."

"I made a pitcher of margarita."

"Even better. You're quite a host. Do you entertain a lot in Austin?"

"Not much." He knew she was asking if he had a girlfriend, if he was with a lot of women, if margaritas and meat were his standard tools of seduction. "I keep pretty much to myself these days."

Delia smiled. "I don't think I believe you."

He opened the refrigerator and proceeded to fix his guest a drink. "It's true. It's just me, my dogs, horse and a few head of cattle. I don't cook for just anyone, sweetheart."

"I'm flattered."

He handed her a thick-stemmed glass filled with the icy drink and she took it carefully, holding it away from the sleeping baby. "How did you do that?"

"What?"

"Put the little monster to sleep."

"A woman's touch," Delia said, giving him another one of those smiles that threatened to knock him to his knees. "That's all she needed."

"Yeah," he said. "Me, too."

Her eyebrows rose. "I doubt that you lack women, Joe. I remember your reputation in high school."

"All lies." He winked at her and retrieved his beer before sitting down at the kitchen table.

"The girls talked about you in gym class. You were quite…experienced." She took a sip of the drink. "Mmm. That's good."

"Girls talk too much," he muttered. "And that was a long time ago. You wouldn't have gone out with me back then."

She looked surprised. "You wouldn't have asked me. You only dated the really cool girls."

"Your mother would have had a stroke if I'd shown up at the front door."

"True." She laughed. "I didn't date much in high school. I was pretty shy."

"And beautiful."

"No." She shook her head. "I wasn't your tall, blond, Texan cheerleader type." She set her glass on the table and leaned forward in the rocker. "I think I'll put Libby to bed."

"You do that and I'll check the steaks." He stood and held the rocker steady for her. Her perfume was light, something that smelled like lilies, he thought. He wanted to dip his lips to her throat and taste her skin. She wore a fitted cotton blouse and a slim denim skirt. Very conservative, his Delia was, but it turned him on to no end. When he was around her he had the overwhelming urge to strip off that proper facade and enjoy the woman underneath.

"I never had the courage to ask you out," Joe admitted, brushing a quick kiss across her lips when she stood. "Until now."

"What happened?"

"I'm older and braver and your mother is miles away." He set his hands on her shoulders.

"Thank goodness."

Joe touched his lips to hers again, because he couldn't help it. He was careful not to touch the sleeping baby, but Delia's mouth needed kissing, that's all there was to it. And the heat that flared between the two of them was unmistakable and deep. He tilted his head to slant his mouth across hers; she opened her lips when his tongue asked her to. This time he kissed because he couldn't help wanting her—not because he was jealous of whatever guy was going to see her on Saturday or to tease her, as he'd done yesterday when he'd gotten out of the shower. He was almost glad she still held Libby, just so he had to exercise a little control. Her unmistakable response and the little sound of disappointment she made when he finally released her just about knocked him off his feet.

"We should have done this sixteen years ago," Joe murmured, looking down into the face of a woman he never thought he'd ever be with.

She shook her head and looked as dazed as he felt. "I would have fallen in love and you would have broken my heart."

"Or the other way around."

"You had a different girl every weekend."

"More gym class lies."

"As my mother would say, where there's smoke there's fire."

"And I'd better check the steaks." He was a little shaken by how fast he'd slipped past common sense and into take-this-woman-to-bed mode.

"You have to take your hands off my shoulders first."

"Yeah." He looked down at the baby pressed against Delia's breasts and reluctantly released his hold. "With luck she'll sleep for hours."

"And Hank?"

"Until morning. Once that kid goes to sleep, that's it."

"So it's just the two of us."

"Yes, sweetheart. I thought it was about time." He winked at her, but turned away before he saw her reaction. She was here and, he told himself, that was all that mattered. For now.

"DINNER'S READY."

Delia took one more look at the sleeping baby and tiptoed out of the room. Hank, wearing Scooby-Doo pajamas and sprawled on the living room couch, slept with his face against a stuffed black dog. "What about Hank?"

Joe found the remote control under another stuffed animal and turned off the cartoon channel. "I'll carry him to bed. The little guy is pretty wiped out."

"He was so scared last night." He should have had his mother to comfort him instead of the stranger from across the street. Delia wished she had the power to drag Martin back to town so Hank would have a mother again.

"Yeah, but the chocolate milk got him through today." Joe bent down and scooped Hank into his arms. "Hey, buddy," he said, keeping his voice low. "I'm taking you into your bed now." The little boy didn't stir, which made Joe chuckle. "He sleeps like a Brown, that's for sure."

She didn't want to know how a Brown slept. She was here for steak and conversation, that's all. She would sip her margarita slowly, she would not let it go to her head, she would behave like a neighbor and not a date.

He returned to the living room and smiled at her. It was that come-hither smile that must have caused any number of her high school classmates to wiggle out of their underwear and haul J. C. Brown into the back seat of their cars. He was tall and dark and lean, with dark green eyes that looked at her as if she'd already removed her panties and thrown them out the window.

"I'm starting to wonder how parents ever get any time alone."

"I don't think they do." She walked toward the kitchen and he followed her.

"My best friend and his wife have five kids, all little. He said they get a sitter once a week and go off to a motel for a few hours."

"Really." She'd never had sex in a motel in her entire life. She would have to start making a list of all the things she'd missed doing. "*Five* children?"

"Sit down and I'll serve us." He moved the rocking chair away from the table and put it in the corner. The oval table was set with blue checked placemats, matching cloth napkins and white plates. In the middle of the table a vase of daisies sat between the salt and pepper shakers and a bottle of barbecue sauce.

"I can't believe you did all this."

He shrugged and held out her chair. "I couldn't take you out anywhere fancy, so this is the next best thing." She watched him place containers of various salads on the table, then cover her plate with a huge steak and a baked potato.

"Just exactly how big are those cows of yours?" She looked down at the steak and wondered how she would eat half of it, never mind the entire thing. It smelled wonderful, like pepper and onions.

Joe sat down across from her. "I was trying to impress you."

"Why?"

He poured white wine into her glass and his, and set the bottle on the table before he answered. "It's a guy thing."

"Well, that explains it then." She picked up her fork and knife and cut a piece of meat.

"I figure this is our first date."

She almost laughed at the satisfied expression on his face. "You do?"

"Yep." Joe toasted her with his wineglass. "And it only took sixteen years, two little kids, a sick mother and a runaway sister to make it happen."

"Don't forget the unfaithful husband." She smiled so he'd know she wasn't suffering from a broken heart.

"I left him out on purpose," he admitted. "He's worth forgetting, right?"

"Absolutely." She remembered that she was supposed to be eating dinner and tasted the steak. "Delicious. Tell me about your ranch."

"It's north of Austin, near Round Rock. I bought the place about six years ago." The pride in his voice was unmistakable. "The barn is new, the house isn't and there's enough land to make a little extra money raising cattle."

"You said you were a part-time rancher. What do you do the rest of the time?"

"I teach."

"You teach," she repeated, uncertain that she had heard him correctly.

"Yeah." Joe gestured toward the bowls between them. "Don't forget to try the various Pecan Hollow specialties."

"What do you teach?"

"History."

"Where?" There was no way on earth she could picture him teaching history to a group of high school students. Not July's legendary bad boy.

"At UT."

"You're a *professor* at the University of Texas?"

"Yes, ma'am. You might say I was a late bloomer, but I did end up going to college and I even studied once in a while. I discovered I liked history—American history—and once I got my doctorate, well, I figured I liked the place enough to stay and get a job. Of course, one of the perks is my season football pass."

"Go Horns."

"Damn right." That dangerous grin again, the one she'd learned to watch out for, flashed her way before he helped himself to the macaroni salad. Too soon, she reminded herself, to like another man this much after only a few months of her divorce. It was one thing to help out a neighbor. And it had been quite natural to share a couple of kisses with Joe, just to see what it would be like to kiss J. C. Brown and feel like a woman again. But liking him? Now *that* could be trouble.

Later, after she'd convinced him to let her help clean up the kitchen, after they'd checked on the sleeping children and before Delia could make her excuses to leave while she still had her clothes on, Joe took her in his arms.

"There," he said, after the kind of kiss that made a woman gasp for air and wonder if her knees still existed. "I couldn't go without doing that much longer."

"I haven't had a lot of experience at this sort of thing," Delia stammered when he took her hand and led her down the hall, to the back of the house. "I'm still not the kind of person who takes her clothes off and has sex for fun, so I think you're wasting your time here, you know?"

"We're going to look at the stars," Joe said. "That's all."

"Stars?" He led her into a dark room, but he didn't turn on the light. She saw the outline of a double bed, but Joe opened a sliding glass door and led her into a sunroom. The windows were open, allowing a warm breeze to cool the air.

"I'll leave the lights off," he said, laughing. "In case you change your mind about the sex." He guided her to a couch padded with thick flowered cushions. "Lean back. Stars, just as I promised."

Delia kicked off her sandals and scooted into the corner of the lounger, which moved. "Oh, it's a glider. My grandmother used to have one of these on her porch."

He sat down next to her, which made the glider sway. "Sometimes I sleep out here. Nice, huh?"

"Very nice." Through the glass panels in the vaulted ceiling, the stars shone in the near-black sky. It was a large room, with a couple of wicker chairs and a round table. In the distance she could see lights from the windows of other Pecan Hollow residents, but in the darkness they seemed miles away, especially since the porch was on the back of the trailer and away from the main road. "It's so quiet back here."

"It's the next best thing to taking a girl to a drive-in movie."

"My mother never let me go." She sighed and leaned back against the cushions. "Do you know any of the constellations?"

"Nothing but the Big Dipper and even then I'm not too sure about it." He took her hand. "What movie did you want to see?"

"What movie—oh," she said, as his thumb caressed her palm. *"Die Hard."*

"Your mother wouldn't let you see *Die Hard*?"

"Not at the drive-in with a boy." She sighed dramatically. "I had a difficult childhood."

He laughed and put his arm around her. "There. That's what we'd do when the movie started. We'd be in the back seat and I'd have a couple of pillows and a blanket in case you got cold. You'd snuggle against me—yeah, like that—and we'd pretend to watch the movie for a while."

"So far so good." She tilted her head back against his arm and looked up to the sky. His fingers caressed her bare shoulder, a lovely tickling sensation. She tried not to laugh when Joe leaned closer and nuzzled her ear, but she couldn't help herself.

"Shhh. You're not supposed to giggle when a guy is putting his best moves on you."

"Sorry." She took a deep breath and looked up at the sky again. "I thought we were watching the movie. I love Bruce Willis. Now what?"

"We're going to forget the earlobe kissing and move right to the cheek," he announced. "Brace yourself." His lips feathered a trail along her jaw to the corner of her mouth. "You're supposed to turn your head and make this easier for me."

"Okay." She did as she was told, but this time she didn't feel like laughing. Her mouth met his in a sweet, tentative kiss that made her feel sixteen again—but only for a moment. Her hands looped around his neck and pulled him closer as he leaned over her, his chest touching her breasts and creating all sorts of havoc in her body. Her tongue mated with his, she breathed with him, held him, wanted him.

And he knew it, damn the man. Delia sensed his surprise, felt his hand at the nape of her neck holding her to him so she couldn't move away even if she wanted to. He stopped, pulled away, took a breath. Those dark green eyes looked into hers.

"I guess you don't want to watch Bruce fight the bad guys," he whispered, and the glider rocked softly.

She shook her head. "I think I know how it's going to turn out."

"Bruce wins?"

"Of course. Why are you frowning?"

"I'd forgotten how small the back seat of a car is." He smiled ruefully. "Come here," he said, and scooped her onto his lap before she could protest.

"I'm too heavy."

"You're perfect. And this leaves both of my hands free in case you let me—"

"Let you what?" It wasn't easy to keep from smiling into his eyes.

"Is this our first date?"

"Oh, yes."

He swore. And shifted her bottom on his lap. Her body, deprived of lovemaking for too many months, was disappointed. Until he took her mouth again. His hands crept to her waist and pulled the hem of her blouse up in one fluid motion.

"You're very good at this," she said. "The rumors were true."

"Shhh. You're wrecking my concentration." He dipped his mouth to the base of her throat and ran his hands beneath her shirt and along the bare skin of her back.

He was wrecking all her vows to stay celibate and sensible. Imagine that, she was making out with J. C. Brown, after all these years.

"Am I supposed to do anything?" she whispered.

"You're supposed to tell me to stop and then we separate for a few minutes while I apologize. But I won't mean it, because—" He moved his hands so that his thumbs touched the sides of her breasts. "Because I got to do this."

"I think that's a fifth or sixth date kind of thing," she said. "But you're the expert."

"Let's say we've been dating for three or four months," he murmured. One hand moved slowly along her breasts and found the clasp between them. He unfastened it with a quick motion and smoothed the fabric away from her skin. It was all she could do not to whimper, which wasn't something a thirty-three-year-old divorced woman would do. She was supposed to be experienced, blasé and oh so casual about sex. But Joe's fingers were doing lovely things to her breasts and nipples, and the heat that radiated between his thighs and hers was becoming too much to ignore. Somewhere a car door slammed, voices in the distance bid "good night," a moth banged at the screen above her head. But the porch felt like a million miles away from anyone.

"Now," he said, his voice rough. "We move to the buttons." He slipped his hands free from her blouse and set to work unbuttoning the front of it until her breasts were exposed to the warm summer night. He eased the blouse from her shoulders and, along with her white bra, tossed it aside. "You can watch the movie if you want."

"I think," she whispered, looping her arms around his neck, "I'd rather watch you. You're definitely very good at this."

"You haven't seen anything yet," he growled, making her laugh until the sound caught in her throat. His lips were on her breast, his hands on her back, his hair tickled her skin and she wondered when she could decently remove his shirt and run her palms along his chest. "These movies can last a long time. But we have all night."

"I'm not spending the night," she whispered. He turned her in his arms and laid her down on her side, wedged against the back cushion. He eased his body alongside of hers and they made the glider move back and forth several times before they were comfortably facing each other, nose to nose. "What are we doing now?"

"Well, I'm going to do this," he said, running his hand up her skirt and along her thigh. "And try not to fall off the swing."

"I always knew I was missing out by not going to

the drive-in." Her face was very close to his, so she touched his jaw. His mouth descended for yet another long, slow, deep kiss that seemed to go on forever while his hand held her thigh and his body leaned into hers, crotch to tingling crotch.

"I knew I should have asked you," he murmured, lifting his mouth a fraction from hers. "But I'd have been too scared to do anything but hold your hand." His fingers inched higher, moving her skirt to her waist. "I'd never have thought of doing this," he said, running his index finger along the edge of her bikini underwear.

She was suddenly very glad she'd worn a skirt. Martin hadn't been much for foreplay, not after the first year of marriage, and she'd never experienced making out on a porch glider. Joe shifted his weight, and his shirt brushed the sensitive skin of her breasts.

"We're crazy," she murmured.

"Don't worry," he said, smiling against her mouth. "I won't do anything you don't want me to."

"That's an old line."

"And I'm an old—"

"Joe, is that you?" A woman's voice penetrated the darkness. "Oh, for heaven's sake!"

"What the hell—" Joe turned his head, lost his balance and fell to the floor. Someone turned the overhead light on, Delia grabbed a pillow to cover her breasts, closed her eyes and groaned.

"*Delia?*" A much too familiar male voice shook

with shock and disapproval. "What do you think you're doing?"

She opened her eyes to see Martin, tanned and angry, standing inside the door to the sunporch. A stunning but tired-looking blonde stood next to him, but her gaze was on her brother, who was scrambling to his feet.

"None of your business," was the only thing she could think of to say to her ex-husband, who hadn't rolled around half-naked with her in quite a few years and—since he'd been on vacation with his new girlfriend—didn't have the right to get stuffy about anyone's sex life.

"Turn off the light, Martin," the woman, her voice deceptively sweet, ordered.

"But Julie, that's my—"

"Now," she demanded, and Martin reached for the light switch and did as he was told. Joe blocked Delia's view when he stood in front of her, but she kept the pillow against her breasts and tried to pull her skirt down.

"Take your time. We'll be in the living room," Julie said, looking as if she wanted to laugh. She grabbed Martin's arm and hauled him back into the house. Joe retrieved her blouse and bra from the floor and handed them to her.

"I'm sorry about that," he said. "I'd hoped Julie would come home soon, but I never thought I'd be so sorry to see her."

"That's okay," she said, not meaning it at all. It

took three tries to untwist her bra, but she managed to get her clothing on. Embarrassment and haste made her clumsy with the buttons.

"Here," he said, reaching toward her. "Let me do that." He buttoned her blouse and then held her waist as if she would run away if he let her go. "Stop looking guilty, sweetheart. We weren't doing anything wrong."

"Of all the people to walk in—" Delia leaned against him, her head on his chest. Hank would think it was Christmas tomorrow morning, little Libby would be in her mother's arms again and Mrs. Brown could get some much-needed rest. But Delia was disappointed.

"Yeah." He stroked her back. "Come on, I'll walk you home."

"No." She pulled away from him and slipped her sandals back on her feet. "You stay here and talk to your sister."

"I wouldn't mind having a few words with Martin, either."

"Don't waste your breath," she warned. "He only hears what he wants to hear."

"He's going to hear *me*," Joe declared, following her to the sliding glass door, left open by the intruders. "Whether he wants to or not." He paused, took her hand to stop her from entering the dark bedroom. "Look, Delia, I'm sorry. About everything. And don't worry, I won't let him hurt you."

"*I* won't let him hurt me," she whispered. "I don't

need you to protect me from Martin and his moral outrage."

"Maybe you do." He sounded angry. "I think you *do* need me, sweetheart, especially now."

Delia straightened her blouse and smoothed her hair, then headed toward the living room. What she needed was to keep her clothes on.

9

JOE WATCHED HER back, whether Delia knew it or not. He gave dumb-ass Martin a warning look, which the man either didn't understand or deliberately ignored.

"Delia, what the heck are you doing here?" He put his hands on the hips of his pressed khaki slacks and the veins in his pudgy neck throbbed above the collar of his yellow polo shirt. He was carrying about thirty extra pounds and his hair was turning gray on the sides. Joe figured he could take him in one well-placed punch.

"I'm sure I already told you that was none of your business," Delia said, heading past him toward the kitchen door.

"You're embarrassing yourself," Martin declared, working himself into a major snit. "Acting like a wanton woman on someone's *porch?* Surely you have more pride."

Joe's hands clenched and he took one step forward. "That's enough, Drummond. Get—"

"You're right," Delia said, cutting off Joe's protest. She paused with her hand on the doorknob. "I should have waited for those nice hotels in Austin and San Antonio, like you and your girlfriend did."

Martin flushed. "We were being discreet."

"Oh, that's what you call it." Delia chuckled. "Whatever." She turned toward Joe, but her smile was cool and polite. "Good night. Thanks again for dinner. And for the movie."

"I'll see you tomorrow," he assured her. Come hell or high water or the hysterics of his crazy sister.

"Where's your car?" Martin wasn't ready to let her go. "I didn't see it in the driveway."

"I walked," she said, and left. Just like that, she was gone and Joe fought the urge to run after her and tell her that Martin had been a fool to stop loving her. And that she was better off without him.

"Walked?"

"Yeah. She lives across the street now." Joe watched Martin's horrified expression as it dawned on him that his ex-wife was living in a trailer park. "In her uncle's trailer."

"She can't do that," he muttered. "What will people think? She knew she could stay in the house until it sold and I gave her enough money—" Martin stopped when Julie reappeared in the living room, the baby against her shoulder.

"Where's Mom? Out playing bingo?" Julie patted her daughter's back and walked over to her boyfriend, who looked nervous at the sight of the tiny child.

"She's in the hospital, Jule," Joe said. "She

wouldn't let me tell you, not that you were answering my calls anyway."

Her eyes filled with tears. "What's the matter?"

"A mild—very mild—heart attack. She's coming home tomorrow." He shoved his hands in his jeans pockets. "She's okay."

"Really?" She sank onto the couch and Martin looked uncomfortable, as if he wasn't used to family dramas.

"Yeah. But she's going to have to rest. She can't take care of the kids full-time anymore." Joe decided the rest of the lecture could wait, because tears started running down Julie's cheeks. No one cried prettier than his sister, he thought, and Martin was a sucker for the sight of a beautiful woman weeping silently. He hurried over to her and sat beside her, his arm around her while he attempted to console her.

"When did it happen?" Julie wiped her eyes with her hands.

"Friday night."

Julie wept harder.

"There, there," the mayor said. "I'm sure your mother is going to be just fine."

"We'll bring her home tomorrow morning." Joe said, watching Martin pull a folded handkerchief from his pants pocket and hand it to Julie, who sniffed prettily. He wondered if the caring boyfriend routine was an act or if Drummond really did care about Julie. He'd ended his marriage for her, but that didn't mean the guy was going to marry her, not a woman with two little kids.

"I feel terrible," Julie muttered, kissing Libby's cheek. "I should have been here."

"Yeah," Joe said. "You've got that right."

"I'd better be going," Martin said.

"Take her for a minute," Julie said, setting the baby in her boyfriend's arms before he could stand up.

"I'm not good with—"

"She's *asleep*, Martin. Just don't wake her up."

"I'll try." Martin looked uncomfortable and chastised. Joe almost felt sorry for him.

Julie wiped her eyes and took a deep breath. "Don't be mad at me, Joe."

"Too late."

She left the couch and led him around the corner, out of sight of Martin. "Please, Joe? I didn't mean to stay away for so long, but we were having such fun and—" His beautiful sister tossed her long hair over her shoulders and whispered, "I'd never been to Las Vegas before."

"That's your excuse?"

Julie shrugged. "It's the truth."

"Don't give me that crap, Jule. Just tell me that you're using birth control so Mom doesn't end up taking care of *three* kids next time you run off."

"Speaking of birth control, what were *you* doing undressing Martin's ex-wife tonight?"

"Martin's ex-wife has been taking care of your kids, Julie. How's that make you feel?" They glared at each other for a long moment, until a wail from Libby broke the silence.

"We'll talk later," Joe said. "Tell your boyfriend it's time to go home."

"Julie, darling?" Martin appeared in the kitchen, the baby fussing in his arms. "I think she wants something, but I don't know what."

"Give her to me," Julie said, turning to soothe her daughter. "Go home, Martin. Call me tomorrow."

Martin fled as if he'd been released from prison.

"He won't last long," Joe muttered, right after the door shut.

"Maybe not," his sister said, patting the baby's back to quiet her. "But right now he might be in love with me. You don't even know what that feels like, being in love, Joe."

He thought about protesting, thought about telling his sister to mind her own business, but she was right. He'd never fallen in love, not really. He'd experienced passion and lust, longing and maybe a crush or two—such as the one he'd had on Delia so many years ago—but the kind of love that made a person do crazy things?

He'd seen love—it had caused his mother to stay with an abusive drunk until the day he died. It had made his brother, rejected by his girlfriend, drink too much and slam his car into a passing train. He'd watched his sister fall in love and get hurt—and pregnant—and he'd seen a couple of his friends crash to earth after meeting the so-called "perfect woman."

Love hurt. And up until this week he didn't need the aggravation.

And then he'd seen Delia on a bar stool, and all of his sensible resolutions went out the window.

Love, huh? So this was what he'd been missing.

IT WAS AFTERNOON before Joe called her name and knocked on the door to the trailer. Delia had been sorting sheet music for hours, but the two cartons of songs were almost empty, their contents preserved in plastic page protectors. All she had to do now was decide what to do with them.

"Come in," she called, and pushed aside a blue binder. "It's open."

"Hi." Joe stepped inside, but he looked uncertain of his welcome.

"Hi." How original. She was smiling at him as if he'd just unbuttoned her shirt again.

"Are you okay?"

"Sure. It's pretty hot today, but—"

"I meant about last night. And Martin and Julie and the whole mess." He sat in the other kitchen chair across from her.

"I'm fine. I was glad to get home, though." And relieved that Joe hadn't followed her home later. She'd had time to think, because she hadn't fallen asleep for hours. She would declare herself a sex-free zone, she would not fall in love with Joe just because he showed her a good time and a heck of a lot of passion. She was vulnerable—her friends had warned her about that. An article in this month's *Redbook* had advised women to experience life on their own for a year or two after a divorce.

"Drummond shouldn't have talked to you that way. I would have hit him for you." He smiled, as if he was joking, but Delia wondered. He thought she needed protecting, which wasn't the case. Not now.

"That's ridiculous. He's not a bad guy, you know. I mean, he has his good points."

Joe's eyes narrowed. "Don't bother to list them for me."

"Okay. On the other hand, he's always been a little too concerned with what people think. And I was as bored with him as he was with me." There. She'd said it, practically announced to the one man who made her blood bubble that she was boring.

"He was sure pissed that you're living in a trailer."

"I wish I'd seen his face." She couldn't help laughing.

"It was almost as good as when Julie made him hold Libby." He looked over at her stack of sheet music. "What are you doing?"

"Saving Uncle Gin's music. I didn't have the heart to throw it out."

He turned one of the binders around and opened it to the first page. "'I've Got All Night to Love You But the Dog Needs Me More'?"

"A personal favorite."

Joe looked back down at the music. "By Horatio *Guinness*?"

"You've heard of him?"

"Yeah. He's part of Texas history, along with Willie and a lot of others who were in Austin back then. I thought he'd died a long time ago."

"Uncle Gin gave away everything he ever earned with his music. He hated performing and he liked being left alone. He had a couple of hits with Willie Nelson, who bought this trailer for him."

"No kidding?"

"He lived off royalties from a few songs that actually got recorded."

"Maybe you should see if a museum wants them."

"Now *you're* kidding."

"No. Someone might be happy to get the Guinness collection. Or you could try to publish them yourself." He flipped through a few more pages and read the titles out loud. "'Take Me Home and Take It Easy,' 'Suck Lemons and Die,' sounds a little hostile. 'Chili Loves Me More Than You So Leave My Beans Alone.'"

"Not exactly mainstream country."

He laughed. "But original. Like his niece." He closed the book and smiled at her. "Have dinner with me tonight. An official second date."

"I don't think so."

"Why not?"

"Because—" She stopped. *Because you're J. C. Brown and I'm out of shape and feeling vulnerable. I have no sexual tricks up my, uh, sleeve and if we had sex I'd disappoint you, and I don't need another kick in the ego, thank you very much.*

"I'm not ready to start dating," she finished, and heard the lie in her own voice as much as Joe did.

"What's the matter, Delia? Are you afraid of what people will say if you're seen in public with one of the no-good Browns?" From the hard expression in his eyes, she realized she hit some kind of nerve.

"That's ridiculous."

"Is it?"

"Look, I'm just not ready for this," she said, fiddling with the stack of sheet music left to put in the last notebook. She couldn't tell him that it would be too damn easy to let him into her life, to let him into her bed and into her heart. And if it was just physical attraction, then once they'd gotten that out of their systems, what was left? Awkward goodbyes and empty promises to get together sometime soon? "I need to be by myself for a while."

"By yourself," he repeated, sliding out of the chair. "Since when? Last night?"

She didn't answer. It really was easier this way, she told herself. Joe looked at her for a long moment and then turned away.

"Call me sometime," he said. "If you're ever in Austin and want to go to the movies."

DELIA CLEANED. She hung tropical print curtains and covered the old couch cushions with yellow denim. She draped red chili pepper lights over the window above the tiny kitchen sink and hung a lime-green shower curtain in the bathroom.

Betty and Hank walked over to say hello one morning. Joe's mother, pale but cheerful, thanked her for helping with the children. Hank beamed and handed her a bouquet of wildflowers and told her his uncle "went away." Well, Delia knew that. His truck hadn't been in the driveway for thirty-seven hours.

She called Kelly and heard about the great man her friend had met—and, she learned, slept with—Saturday night. She called Carol and listened to her describe the merits of her cousin, an accountant in Austin who was recently divorced. She agreed with both of her friends that she needed to get a life, and that going out and having fun would cheer her up fast.

Oh, yes, she'd said. Good idea. Sure, she'd told Kelly. We'll do something on the Fourth. Yes, she'd said, that would be fun. And what better way to illustrate her happiness with single life? She was happy, though no one believed her. She was supposed to have a broken heart, but what she had was the strange feeling that at some point in her life she'd taken a wrong turn. Maybe she'd been destined for Pecan Hollow all along. Maybe she should have finished college, but majored in art. She could have been one of those temperamental artists, well respected and profiled in Texas magazines. Instead she'd fallen in love with the first man who told her she was beautiful. She'd stepped right out of her mother's house and into someone else's and she'd foolishly believed she'd been guaranteed a happy ending.

She didn't tell either one of her friends about her

brief flirtation with J. C. Brown. Neither one would have believed that the wild high school kid had turned into a college professor, rancher and family man. And neither one would believe her if she told them that she'd been half-naked with him the other night.

They would think she was joking. Saint Delia and J. C. Brown?

Never in a million lifetimes.

"MY GOODNESS," was all Georgia could say when she saw the inside of the trailer Thursday morning. Though it was overly bright and a bit too tropical for Georgia's taste, at least it wasn't filled with Browns. *That* had been a day she wouldn't soon forget.

"I decided to brighten up the place, turn it into a studio."

"A studio," Georgia echoed, walking into the living room. Yes. Delia's endless boxes of beads were on the shelves, along with her various jewelry books and thick collection of beading magazines. Delia's special magnifying lamps were stationed beside and above a corner work area, next to the television. The sofas, once a hideous brown, now made Georgia glad she'd kept her sunglasses on. "How nice. Why yellow?"

"I needed color."

"Yes," Georgia said, nodding politely. "I can see that." She could also see Julie Brown playing ball with her son across the road. "How is Betty Brown doing? I heard she was out of the hospital."

"She came home Monday and is doing fine. I

guess she just needed to be on the right medication."
Delia handed her a cup of coffee and Georgia
squeezed into the little booth and set the mug on the
Formica table.

"This is all very nice," she said. Too nice, she worried. Delia looked as if she was settling into this
gaudy little trailer park, for goodness sake. "So, what
have you been doing with yourself?"

"I've met some of the neighbors." She took a sip
of coffee. "At the Laundromat here."

"You could do your laundry at my house. You certainly don't have to traipse down the road to use the
public washing machines."

"And I've been working on my jewelry." She
looked pleased. "I'm going to call the stores and tell
them I'm taking orders again."

"Oh?"

"And I've been organizing Uncle Gin's music into
notebooks. He certainly wrote a lot of songs."

"Have you heard any news on the house?"

"You mean, if it's sold yet?"

Georgia nodded.

"I haven't called the real estate agent to ask."

"But the money—" Georgia said. "I'm sure you
don't want to live in a trailer for the rest of your life."

Delia smiled. "It's not that bad, Mother. Think of
the money I'm saving."

"Yes, but—"

"And since I don't know what I want to do with
the rest of my life, this is as good a place as any to be."

"Have you thought anymore about seeing a doctor?" She pulled the paper with the psychiatrist's name and phone number out of her pants pocket. "I heard that this man is very good."

"I don't need a doctor." Her daughter looked as if she wanted to burst into giggles, something that Georgia did not think was appropriate under the circumstances.

"Be serious, darling. You've had a lot of life changes in the last eight months. You've lost your husband—"

"No big loss," Delia interjected. "Not anymore."

"And your house."

"It was never really mine."

"Money."

"I'm not destitute. Not yet." She waved her hand toward the shelves of beads she used to make jewelry and flowers. "I could make a business out of my beading. There are a couple of stores in San Marcos that said they'd take anything I would make. I'll become an artist." She laughed. "And this will be my studio."

This was not the picture Georgia had painted of her daughter's future. She thought Delia would move in with her, they would share breakfasts and suppers and watch the news together. It would be great fun having her sweet-natured daughter as company. But she didn't recognize the woman seated across from her in Gin's trailer, now decorated like a South Pacific island or a Jimmy Buffett bar.

"A cruise," Georgia said, saying the first thing that

popped into her head. "I thought we could go on a cruise together. The ships leave out of Galveston, you know, and go all sorts of places. Wouldn't that be fun?"

"You want to go on a cruise with your crazy, destitute, divorced daughter?"

"Who else?" They both laughed. "We'd shop, go to the shows each night on the ship, take one of those rides in a raft—or maybe not. Maybe we'd be better off touring one of those Mexican ruins with the pyramids in the middle of the jungle."

"Mother, I can't picture you in the jungle."

"We'll have an adventure." She would brave snakes and mosquitoes and seasickness to see Delia happy and normal again. She'd heard that J. C. Brown had left town, thank goodness, so maybe now Delia would stop befriending riffraff and return to being sensible.

"I'll think about it," Delia promised.

"I imagine you could find a lot of interesting beads in Mexico." There. Now she would go home and arrange for someone to come to the house and paint Delia's bedroom yellow.

Pale yellow.

JOE TOLD HIMSELF he only came back to town to check on his mother, but since he talked to her every day he knew damn well she was doing fine. Never better and, yes, she was taking her medication and watching her diet. According to Mom, Julie was now Mother of the Year and Martin the Mayor had been very helpful with Hank. He has two sons of his own, his mother had told Joe as if that meant that Drummond was automatically going to offer his services as stepfather and husband.

He'd arrived at Pecan Hollow in time to see Julie and Hank leave for the fireworks and his mother setting the table for a card party with some of the neighbors.

"We're too old for fireworks," she'd said. "Libby's asleep and I'm feeling fine. You go have a good time."

Delia's trailer was dark, her driveway empty. She was somewhere having a good time of her own, though Joe didn't want to think too much about that. She'd turned him down and she'd had her reasons, whatever they were. He had his pride and his own life to get on with.

Trouble was, he'd kept thinking about Delia. Wondering if she ever thought of him. Wondering what she'd think of his place, if she'd ever knock on his door and ask for a tour. If anyone in July was making moves on her. If she was staying away from strawberry daiquiris and the Cottonwood Bar.

The crowd at the annual Fourth of July gathering was partying pretty hard when he arrived. The annual celebration took place behind the high school, so those who wanted to watch fireworks were settled in the bleachers with their families, while local bands took turns entertaining the dancers in the football field. Booths selling all sorts of food, bars selling drinks and stands with American flags and this year's "July's Fourth of July" T-shirt ringed the field. The outdoor lights were on and the crowd waited for it to be dark enough to start the fireworks.

Joe looked around for Julie and Hank, but it was too dark to spot them. He bought a beer and stood at the edge of the makeshift dance floor and wondered why the hell he'd bothered to come to town at all.

"Hey, J.C.," someone said. "How ya doin'?"

"Fine. You?"

"Not bad." The man—someone Joe vaguely remembered from high school—disappeared into the crowd and Joe looked around for the woman he wanted to see. He'd only come for one reason and that reason was dancing with another guy, a young kid in his twenties who looked as if he'd won the lottery. He also looked pretty drunk. He swung Delia around, then tucked her against him in a sloppy two-step that concluded with an obscene motion of the kid's hips.

Guess Saint Delia was having a good time at the party. Joe frowned and told himself he was better off going back to Austin and letting Delia enjoy being a single woman. He watched her laugh and back away, but the young cowboy didn't listen. His hands slid down Delia's back and cupped her buttocks so that she couldn't get away from him. Joe edged closer, his view blocked by a large man wearing a Stetson and twirling his granddaughter. By the time Joe avoided three young women, their jean shorts well below their contoured abdomens, and a fat kid carrying a cardboard tray piled high with tacos, he'd lost sight of Delia and her horny dancing partner.

The woman needed a bodyguard. And the worst part of it was that she didn't know it. She thought she could dance around in a short denim skirt and a little white T-shirt and not have guys falling all over her. He'd never met a woman who had less of a clue as to how damned attractive she was.

Of course it was none of his business if she wanted to be groped on a plywood dance floor by a guy ten years younger. He caught sight of her again, only this time she was grappling with the cowboy, who must have thought that a woman fighting him was a turn-on, because he didn't seem at all upset. He even looked like he was having fun.

Delia smiled, but it was her polite smile, and she was trying to move out of the guy's embrace. The stupid kid looked surprised and confused all of a sudden when Joe's hand clapped him on the shoulder.

"The lady's tired of you groping her," Joe growled. "Take your hands off her. Now."

"Hey, man, we're havin' fun here—" He shut up, getting the message in Joe's expression. "Yeah, okay." He tipped his hat in an exaggerated gesture of courtesy toward Delia, then staggered into the crowd.

"What are you doing here?"

"I was going to ask you the same thing." He took her into his arms as naturally as if they'd been dancing for hours. The band began an old George Jones tune, slow and sad, with just the right beat for dancing close.

"I'm here with friends."

"Friends? Like rodeo boy there?"

"Female friends," she informed his shoulder. As if to prove it, she waved at a stunning redhead holding hands with a stocky rancher next to the cotton candy machine. "We're having a nice time, enjoying the party."

"Yeah. You were having one hell of a good time. I could see that from the way that kid was grabbing you and you were trying to get away."

"He'd had too much to drink." She sighed and glanced up at him. "He didn't mean anything."

"I figured you needed some help." She felt good in his arms, all warm and soft and sweet. Her hair brushed his lips and he fought the desire to carry her off and make love to her under the bleachers.

"You figured wrong. I had just kicked him when you came over." She stopped dancing and showed him the pointed toe of her cowboy boots. "See? That's a lethal weapon."

"That wouldn't stop most guys intent on getting what they want." Hell, that kid could have manhandled her across the field and to the parking lot without her having a chance to defend herself. Folks would have assumed it was some kind of lovers' quarrel and Delia would have been at that guy's mercy. He eased her back into his arms. "Sweetheart, a beautiful woman can't be too careful."

"Hey, man, it's my turn." A hand clamped on Delia's shoulder and Joe saw that the kid was back, this time looking ugly and determined. He'd had time for another shot of liquor to boost his courage, Joe supposed. And he'd brought a friend along for support. Joe braced himself for a couple of ugly minutes.

"Get lost," Joe said. "And take your hand off the lady."

"I saw her first," the kid drawled. "You—you gotta go get your own woman."

"Go away," Delia said, but she looked scared now and shrugged off the hand that held her. That was all Joe needed to see. No one was going to put that look in her eyes and get away with it. Joe thrust her behind his back and hoped she'd have the sense to stay put.

"I don't want trouble," Joe told them, meeting each man's inebriated gaze. He said the only thing that would make this end without having to hit anyone. "The lady is my wife."

The kid held up his hands. "Whoa, man, I didn't know. I thought—well, hell, it's a party and—" He looked confused, having forgotten what he was going to say. "No hard feelin's."

"No problem." Joe watched them stagger to the edge of the dance floor before he turned to Delia and took her into his arms again. They danced in silence until the song came to an end and she withdrew from his embrace.

"Thanks." She looked up at him with those big hazel eyes guaranteed to make him wish they were alone. "You were right—I needed help." She didn't look too pleased to admit it.

"What are you doing, Delia? Showing Martin you don't care?"

She shook her head. "I get tired of people feeling sorry for me. You should hear them when they think I can't hear. *Poor Delia,* they say. *Such a nice girl and such a shame what happened to her.*" Delia shrugged. "I know, I shouldn't care, but—"

"What people say hurts," he finished for her.

"Yes."

"Come on," Joe said, taking her hand in his. He was suddenly tired of the noise, the people, the band's loud rendition of the "Yellow Rose of Texas." He didn't want to spend the rest of the night without her. She couldn't hold her liquor and she had something to prove, a bad combination and a recipe for trouble.

"Where?"

"Home. If you're so determined to have sex with a stranger, you might as well do it with me."

10

"SEX WITH A STRANGER? A few minutes ago we were married." She didn't mind leaving the dance floor. And her heart had been pounding faster ever since Joe walked up to her and banished her dance partner. He'd returned to July—maybe to check on Julie, probably to see how his mother was feeling, but whatever his reason, she was glad he'd come along when he had and rescued her from the drunk. The second time the young man had appeared had been frightening until Joe started in with the "wife" explanation. No one had referred to her as a wife for a long time, thank goodness, but at least it had worked to stop a fight. Now Joe was talking about having sex instead of being arrested by one of July's deputies.

"You're going to drive me crazy," she heard him mutter. Delia managed to wave goodbye to Kelly, who gave her a thumbs-up and a big grin. "Which car, yours or mine?"

"Where are we going?" She started to wonder if he was serious. And her first thought was *oh, please*. And then, *oh, no*.

"Your place or mine. Doesn't matter to me as long as we're out of here. And out of here now."

"Yours as in *Austin?*"

"If we have to, but I'd rather not waste two hours driving."

"Mine, then, but I haven't agreed to the sex. And you're not exactly a stranger."

He ignored her comments and kept walking through the dark, his hand tight around hers. "Where's your car?"

"Far away. We're going to miss the fireworks." She hurried to keep up with him, despite the fact that she could hardly see anything now that they were leaving the football field.

"Please tell me you're not drunk," he muttered. "I still have some standards, even in July."

"I am not drunk," she retorted. "I'm stumbling because I can't see. And I had one rum and Coke, that's it. I'm perfectly aware that you're dragging me across a field with the intention of seducing me and I'm also quite capable of telling you 'no.'"

He stopped in the grassy parking area west of the football field and kissed her like a man starving for the taste of her lips. His hands slid down her back and lower, to cup her bottom and pull her against his arousal. And an impressive arousal it was, Delia realized, as her body reacted by melting into him.

He'd meant it about the sex, then.

His tongue delved into her mouth, touched, stroked, burned with a need so hot that it was all

Delia could do to stay on her feet. Her boots kept her grounded and her hands clutched his shoulders or her body would have collapsed to the dirt. And still Joe held her, his large hands holding her to him as if he wanted her to know what he was feeling.

She knew, all right.

Joe finally lifted his mouth and drew a ragged breath. "Couldn't wait."

"No."

"Delia, the car?"

She closed her eyes and tried to remember something as mundane as where she'd left the Cadillac. "It's in the teachers' parking lot."

"Where's that?"

Delia pointed toward the new addition to the school. "Over there."

Somehow they managed to weave through parked cars and tailgate parties, past groups of teenagers and excited families, to the paved parking lot. The first burst of fireworks lit up the sky behind them just as they reached the car, but neither one paid the least bit of attention.

"The keys are inside," she said, when he opened the passenger door for her.

"You left the key—never mind. I forget what it's like to live in a small town." He shut the door and went around to the driver's side. Delia plucked the keys from under the floor mat and handed them to him when he slid behind the wheel.

"I'd kiss you now," he said, looking more like the

devilish J. C. Brown she remembered. "But I'm not sure we wouldn't end up in the back seat. And I'm too old for back seats."

"It might be fun." It was certainly something she'd never done before.

He shook his head and turned the key in the ignition. "I have visions of your mother knocking on the car window and telling me she's going to have me arrested."

"You don't have anything to worry about. She's manning one of the chili dog booths with her church group."

"Then we need to be miles away." Joe put the Cadillac in reverse and within minutes they were on their way out of town, fireworks bursting in the night sky behind them. Delia turned to look.

"What about your truck?"

"I'll get it in the morning." He rolled down the window and let the cool air rush into the car. "Pecan Hollow?"

"Yes," Delia said, feeling like a teenager about to do something wonderful and illicit. "This is a one-night stand, isn't it?"

He glanced toward her and frowned. "Why would you say that?"

"I've always wanted to have one." She ignored his soft curse. "But I have to warn you."

"About what?"

"I'm really out of practice." There. She'd admitted it. "And I don't go to a gym. And—"

"Stop," he interrupted. "Please."

"I thought you should know."

"Maybe we should have stayed in the parking lot," he muttered. "We'd be naked by now and you wouldn't be obsessing over your body. *I'd* be obsessing over your body, which is the way it should be, sweetheart."

"You could always pull over," she said sweetly.

He stepped on the gas instead. "We're six minutes away. Could you talk about something else other than sex?"

She laughed and rolled down her window. "Seen any good movies lately?"

"Witch." But he smiled when he said it and his right hand reached over and took hers. "I missed you."

She'd missed him, too, but for the life of her she didn't know why she felt as if her world righted itself every time she saw him. There was something about the man that made her want to hold him close and inhale his scent and wait for his slow smile to brighten those stark features and make his green eyes turn up at the outside corners.

"Three minutes to go," he announced and winked at her. "If you want to take your underwear off now we could save some time when we get to the trailer."

"Seduction at its finest," Delia murmured, trying not to laugh out loud again. "No wonder you were so popular in high school."

"One mile and you're mine."

"Sounds like one of Uncle Gin's song titles."

"One mile and you're mine. Just past the neon sign," he said. *"I'll find you with your clothes off and that's when I'll make you pine."*

"That was really, really awful."

"One of my college roommates was a poet. I made him crazy." He squeezed her hand and released it in order to turn the car into Pecan Hollow.

He was making her a little crazy, too. Her stomach did nervous flips as the headlights flashed on the silver trailer before Joe parked the car and turned off the lights. Behind them Betty's double-wide was lit up like it was Christmas and down the street someone was having a party. She stepped out of the car at the same time Joe did; their doors slammed in unison.

"You can change your mind," he said, his face unreadable in the darkness. "But I hope you don't."

"Me, too."

They walked toward the steps, illuminated by a small light above the door. Delia reached down and took the key from under the new welcome mat and unlocked the door. Inside the trailer the air was cool and dry, but a faint chili aroma still lingered.

"The ghost of Uncle Gin," Delia said, wondering if she should turn on the lights or offer Joe a drink or drag him into the bedroom. "No matter how much air freshener I use I can't—"

His hands closed on her shoulders and his warm breath tickled the back of her neck before he smoothed her hair and kissed the sensitive spot behind her ear. She forgot what she was going to say.

Joe turned her around to face him. "It's hopeless."

"What is?"

"You and me trying to stay away from each other." He gazed down at her and smiled. "I'm not sure what's going on," he said, "but I like it."

"Lust," she whispered. "I think that's what it's called."

"Hmm." He brushed his lips across hers in a slow, teasing motion. "You could be right."

"Like I'm such an expert."

"Yeah." He cradled her face with his hands. "And so beautiful."

"Don't." She didn't want extravagant compliments. Not from Joe.

"Don't tell you that you're beautiful and that I want to make love to you for hours, until we're too tired to move when the sun comes up?"

"Hours?"

"Hours, days, weeks, months. Take your pick."

"Well, okay." She was still smiling when he kissed her again, though this time was no gentle brushing of lips, but a blissful invasion of her mouth that reminded her of what lay ahead. His tongue explored and teased, while she matched him with her own need to taste and savor the flavor of him.

Somehow they managed to walk down the thankfully short distance to the bedroom. Joe eased her onto the bed and followed her down until he lay beside her in a tangle of arms and legs and need on the wide mattress.

"I feel as if we're getting away with something," she whispered after he'd tugged her cowboy boots off.

"Is that good or bad?" He pulled her shirt from the waistband of her skirt and slid his hands under the cotton to touch the lace that covered her breasts.

"I don't know, but I like—oh!" He'd unclasped the front hook of her bra and his fingers swept over her skin, freeing her breasts from the confining material. He helped tug her T-shirt over her head and tossed it aside, while she reached for his shirt and started in on the buttons. Two popped off the fabric near the bottom of the shirt, when she'd lost patience and only wanted to feel his skin under her fingertips. The shirt flew to the floor.

His mouth was on her breast, teasing the nipple into an aching hardness that intensified the ache between her thighs. His hands bunched her skirt to her waist and then touched her underwear.

And stopped.

"My God," he breathed, his fingers tracing the line of the panties over her hip to her exposed buttock. "Delia Drummond is wearing a thong?"

"It was a divorce present." She'd finally decided to wear it tonight, an act of courage made possible by going out under the cover of darkness. "Don't laugh."

"Laugh?" He lowered his head to her hip and kissed the bare skin below the lace trim. "Never."

It was the feel of his mouth along her upper thigh that ended any rational thought Delia might have had. She was lost when he unzipped her skirt, thrilled when the fancy white thong joined her clothes on the floor and completely ecstatic when Joe removed his jeans and joined her in bed.

At the other end of the park someone shot off fireworks, but in the dark bedroom of the trailer Delia and Joe didn't notice. The bedcovers were pushed back, Delia's legs entwined with Joe's and she wondered how she'd ever survived without having this man's hard body against hers. He suckled her breasts, she slid her hand down his side and forward, to the hard length of him so hot against her abdomen. His fingers—those long hard fingers—worked hot magic between her thighs, sliding into her vagina with practiced strokes and bringing her perilously close to orgasm. But right now she wanted, needed more than teasing fingers and she urged his body closer.

"We have all night," he said, his voice gruff with passion. "If you touch me like that again I'm going to have to be inside you."

"Good."

He kissed her hard, then moved off the bed for a second. She heard him rustling through his jeans and then he returned to the bed, a condom in his hand.

"Thanks," she said, embarrassed that she hadn't said something about protection. It was something a single woman should be prepared for. She'd read that in *Cosmo* and she should have made a note to buy condoms, not that she had plans to have sex every weekend, but a woman never knew. "I should have—"

"I always—"

"Really, I—"

He stopped her apology with a kiss, slid alongside of her and turned her to face him, their heads on the pillow. He urged her onto her back, braced himself on his elbows and nudged her willing thighs apart. He filled her slowly, easing in and out of her slick vagina in moves guaranteed to make her want more. And she did, the rush of pleasure taking her breath away. Her hands clutched his hips and he filled her completely then, buried inside her as if that was where he belonged.

She met his smile. "That," she said, her body adjusting to the size of him, "feels so very good."

Joe closed his eyes for a brief second and withdrew half his length, then plunged into her again. "You're perfect, you know."

"*This* is perfect," she said, tilting her hips slightly to bring him deeper into her. He'd spent a long five days wondering what it would be like to be buried to the hilt inside of her, but his imagination hadn't done justice to the reality. She was tight around him, creamy and hot, and he knew that no other woman would ever feel like this. He'd been waiting for Delia, he realized, waiting to make love to her with everything he could give. He watched her face as he moved within her, listened to the little moans of pleasure when they found each other's rhythm and moved toward heaven.

She came first, which led him to his own release,

an explosion that seemed to come from the very base of his spine. It was like nothing else he'd ever experienced, he realized some moments later, when he was still trying to catch his breath against Delia's neck. Her hair lay in tangles on the pillow and he saw that her eyes were closed. He could feel her heart pounding beneath his chest, and wondered if she had experienced the same kind of joy as he. He was surprisingly still hard, still inside of that tight warmth. It would be polite to retreat, but he had no intention of moving off the bed. With little encouragement and not much time, he would make love to her again.

This time, slowly.

Delia turned, opened her eyes. Smiled. Wriggled as if she liked the feel of him inside her. "Don't go."

"No," he agreed. Leaving the bed hadn't occurred to him.

"Good."

He planted a playful kiss on her mouth. "I should have taken you up on your offer to have—what did you call it? Wild and crazy sex?" At her nod he continued. "Doing it in the pool in the middle of the afternoon with a drunk suburban divorcée would have been one hell of a challenge."

"The neighbors would have been shocked. I like this better." She waved her arm toward the high windows covered with miniblinds. "No one knows we're here."

"Is that so important?" He slid out of her, got rid of the condom and returned to the bed. He lay on his back, clasped his hands behind his head and stared at the ceiling. Sure as hell, this night had been too perfect.

"I meant I was glad we're not going to be interrupted. That we have our privacy without the whole town knowing our business." She leaned over him. "It's not what you think, what you said last time, that I didn't want to be seen with you. Why *would* you think something like that?"

"Easy. Not too many people in July would think I was good enough for you. Not sixteen years ago and not now." He turned on his side and so did Delia, so they faced each other in the darkness. Then he drew the edge of the sheet over her shoulder, just in case she was cold. Delia moved closer, tucked her head in the crook of his arm and sighed with something that sounded like contentment.

"It's awful," she said softly, "not being good enough."

"Sweetheart, could we talk about something else?" He ran his hand along her shoulder, amazed that he could touch her naked body with such ease. He brushed a palm over her breasts and felt her shiver.

"You're not the only one, you know. I used to think I wasn't a good enough wife or a good enough stepmother. I'm over that now, though." Her body, warm and naked and all his for the night, nestled against him. He couldn't imagine any man thinking that this woman lacked anything.

"Smart thinking. That husband of yours was an ass."

"But why do you care what people think? You're not the same person you were years ago."

"It's not something I think about a lot." He paused, wondering how to explain growing up poor, scared and wild without sounding like he was feeling sorry for himself. "My father was a mean drunk and everyone knew it, figured his sons would be just like him. Whenever I'm in July I figure everyone's waiting to see what wild-ass thing I'm going to do next."

"I was kind of wondering that myself." Her hand wandered from his chest to his hip then lower, to the part of his body that lay rigid along her stomach. She encased him with her fingers and tugged ever so gently.

"Want to know what I'm thinking about?"

"That I'm easily aroused?"

"Well, yes, thank goodness." She laughed, but her hand continued pleasuring him. "And I was also thinking that I like the wild side of you, too."

"Sweetheart," he groaned, growing painfully large. "I love you and your hot little hand, but a few more seconds of that and I'm going to embarrass myself."

She stopped, but her fingertips ran the length of him as if she was testing his hardness. "So, J. C. Brown, are you ready to have wild and crazy sex with a love-starved divorcée?"

"Love starved, huh?" He rolled onto his back and

took her with him. She straddled his abdomen and leaned forward for his kiss. "I can fix that."

And that was the last time Joe spoke for a long, long time.

11

HE HAUNTED HER long after she should have been asleep. Delia listened to his even breathing, touched his calf with her toes, rested her head on her pillow and marveled at the sight of his dark hair so close to hers.

Joe had made love to her a third time with exquisitely slow hands and a way of touching her that made her face grow warm in the remembering. He had wriggled down the length of her body, left a trail of hot tickling kisses to the very core of her. And he had made her laugh, before he took her breath away.

The man wasn't shy. Sometime in the middle of the night they had showered together, no small feat considering the size of the shower stall. He had soaped her, using his hands instead of a washcloth. He had held her against him, her head on his shoulder and the water pouring down along his chest, while his fingers gently traced the curves of her body and lathered her skin. She'd been too exhausted, too enthralled to do anything but let the sensations—and the warm water—wash over her. With her eyes closed and her lips touching his neck, she'd come again.

She'd intended to return the favor, but he'd fallen asleep. There would be plenty of time tomorrow, she assured herself, though she only half-believed it. After all, she was not the most worldly or sophisticated woman in July. She didn't know how these things were done. Was it too domestic to cook Joe breakfast or was it considered polite to offer? Would he leave before dawn, while she was asleep, and slip across the street to the guest bedroom? Or would he help himself to coffee, thank her for the evening and then make one of those meaningless promises to "call." She wished she'd thought to ask Kelly how these things were done.

Love was complicated.

The thought chilled her. Love? Why was she thinking about love? She didn't want to fall in love with anyone, yet this crazy feeling of happiness kept building. Until, looking at Joe's profile, she wanted nothing more than to slide her body against his and stay that way forever.

Forever was not a good idea. She would have to act casual in the morning. As if making love to Joe was great fun, but nothing more. She would reorganize the bins of antique Czech beads, sorting by color *and* size. She would finish repairing the beaded Victorian purse she'd found at a yard sale last summer. And if Joe lured her back into the bedroom, she would race him to the bed.

Being single and carefree definitely had its advantages, as long as a woman didn't fall in love.

JOE COULD HAVE opened his eyes, but he decided that it was better to stay completely still and enjoy the feel of Delia's body tucked against his. It had to be morning, because he felt like he'd slept for hours. He felt pretty damn good, too, like a man who'd had his greatest wish come true.

He sure as hell didn't regret hauling her out of town before the fireworks started. She would have only gotten in trouble there on the dance floor, no matter how much she insisted she could take care of herself.

He didn't believe it. And he was damn glad he'd arrived in time to stop her being mauled. *My wife*, he'd said. The word had shocked him, coming out of his mouth as easily as his own name. He'd never really thought too much about getting married and settling down.

He hadn't thought about it at all, even when he'd considered taking the children and his mother and heading back to Austin. There was no room in his life for a wife, someone who would expect more than he could give. Someone who would insist on sweet talk and devotion, someone he was tied to for the rest of his life—barring the unexpected, naturally.

He'd wanted to believe that love lasted forever, but then again, sometimes that wasn't a good thing. All he had to do was look at his mother to remind himself that love didn't always have happy endings, that some folks paid too high a price when they fell in love.

Joe looked at the sleeping woman beside him. The

white sheet covered her body from the cool breeze of the air conditioner, but now he knew what that body felt like. And tasted like. And how it responded to his.

Walking out of here this morning was going to be damn near impossible. He'd been a little bit in love with Delia since he was a kid and now? Well, now he was a grown man who still knew what he wanted. Joe leaned closer to her and placed a soft kiss on her perfect mouth before he closed his eyes and gave in to the temptation of sleeping just a while longer.

"SHE WON'T SEE ME!"

"Shh," Delia said, and Joe sat up in bed as if the room was about to be invaded. Who in hell was making such a racket? The male voice, though, was familiar. Uncomfortably familiar.

"Why? You have company?" The man snorted as if he'd made a joke, but when he spoke again his voice was lower. "She dumped me, Delly. After everything I did for her."

Joe wished Delia hadn't closed the bedroom door. He'd give a lot to see Martin Drummond's face when he discovered a man in Delia's bed. It was tempting to climb out of bed and walk into the kitchen, but he hesitated. He suspected Delia wouldn't appreciate him making his presence known.

"Do *not* call me 'Delly.'" *Big mistake, Martin.* Joe grinned.

"But—"

"And I don't want to hear about your girlfriend,"

Delia said. "I don't want you coming over here, either. Unless you're here to tell me you sold the house and you're going to hand over a check."

"Gee, when did you get so mean?" There was the sound of water in the sink and then Joe heard the coffee grinder.

"I think it came on suddenly," she said. "Just this morning."

"There's a lot of that going around." Martin sighed. "I've been across the street. Julie won't talk to me—at least her mother said she was sleeping."

"It's not even nine o'clock. Maybe she was up with the baby last night."

"She took Hank home after the fireworks and then she went out dancing. Without me."

Obviously Julie wasn't as in love as she said she was, Joe decided. Not anymore.

"You've never been much of a dancer," Delia pointed out. "And the kinds of parties you like don't include bars and country music."

"I saw her leave the Creek bar. With a man."

"So now you're a stalker?"

"I'm crazy about her. So sue me. You're making coffee? Good." Joe heard a chair move, as if the guy was rearranging the furniture for his comfort. "I'll give Julie some time to wake up and wait here."

"Go back to your condo, Martin. Go have breakfast with your daughter and read the paper or something. You're not going to hang around here and cry on my shoulder about your love life." There was silence for a long moment and Joe smelled the coffee brewing.

"This place looks like a cheap bar." Martin couldn't take a hint and leave, which meant it was time Joe considered making an entrance.

"That's the look I was going for, all right." Ah, yes, Joe thought. Sarcasm from the little lady.

"I want you to move back home."

Joe was off the bed and into his jeans in less than thirty seconds.

"I'm living *here* now," he heard Delia reply, so he stopped to listen.

"You're doing this on purpose," Martin muttered. "Staying in a run-down trailer park to embarrass me in front of everyone in town."

"I think you've done that all by yourself," Delia pointed out.

"Please. Let's not relive the past. Move back in the house until the place is sold. We agreed that would be the best for everyone." Martin's voice held more confidence than was smart. Joe zipped up his jeans and sat on the bed to put on his boots. He might have to kick the son of a bitch down the stairs.

"I changed my mind. I like living here a lot better than I did on Lincoln Street."

"Because you're closer to your new boyfriend?" There was a sneer in Martin's voice that Joe didn't care for. He stood and walked over to the bedroom door. "Really, Delia, you could have done a lot better for yourself than J. C. Brown. He's only out for one thing, and you know darn well what that is."

The doorknob moved silently, the door swung inward.

"Maybe that's what I'm after, too," Delia said. Joe saw that she was dressed, her hands on her hips as she faced her ex-husband, who now stood in the kitchen as if he was waiting to be offered a cup of coffee.

"But—" Martin's mouth dropped open as Joe walked into the kitchen, but his chest puffed out like he owned the place.

"You were saying?" Joe pretended a nonchalance he didn't feel, just in case the jerk decided to shut up and get out.

"Oh, great." Martin rolled his eyes at Delia. "And I thought it couldn't get any worse. But you've actually had *sex* with him?"

"Yes. I've had sex. Hot sex. Wild sex. Sweaty, passionate, upside-down sex. *Casual* sex, Martin."

"This—this isn't like you, Delia."

She lifted her chin in a proud gesture. "I know. Isn't it great?"

Casual sex? Joe wasn't sure he'd agree that what happened last night could be described as "casual." And he didn't like having his sex life discussed, either, damn it.

"Delia—" Martin's face flushed. He looked like he might have a heart attack. "He's using you."

"Get out," she said, and poked a finger in his chest. "Now."

"And leave you to shack up with J. C. Brown like the town slut? No way. You'll be the laughing-stock—" His words stopped abruptly when Joe's fist connected with his mouth. It was a satisfying crunch, though painful. Joe hadn't hit anyone for a long time, but he hadn't forgotten how. He packed a pretty good wallop in his right fist and Martin staggered backward until he hit the kitchen door.

"Joe!"

"You bathard." Martin put his hand up to his mouth.

"The lady told you to leave," Joe said, flexing his fingers in case he had to hit Drummond again. "So leave."

"You're crazy," the man muttered, shooting Joe a look that promised revenge.

Joe met his gaze. "You need help down the steps?"

Martin, his nose bloodied, turned around and left. Joe faced Delia, whose fingers gripped the gray-speckled Formica counter. "Sweetheart? Are you okay?"

"What have you done?" She looked at him as if she thought he was some kind of idiot.

Joe shrugged and opened the refrigerator. Inside was the freezer, with its assorted ice cube trays. He'd need to keep the swelling down if he wanted to be able to use his hand tomorrow. "I got him to stop bothering you."

"You shouldn't have hit him."

"He insulted you."

She shook her head. "It's not worth it."

"Hey, a man protects his woman." He grinned at

her and set the ice cube tray on the counter. "Can I get a cup of that coffee?"

"No. I'm going to drive you to town so you can get your truck and then you're going to go back to Austin before the police come."

"Police?" He dumped the ice cubes onto a dish towel, then wrapped it around his knuckles. "I didn't *kill* him, Delia. I just punched him in the mouth. Which, by the way, he had coming."

"You punched a *lawyer* in the mouth, Joe. Martin will be filing assault charges as soon as he gets back to town."

Joe couldn't help laughing. She stood there looking so serious and worried, as though he couldn't take care of himself. "He's just mad about Julie, that's all. I'm glad she got rid of him, but Mom's going to be heartbroken. She thought she was finally going to get a respectable son-in-law."

"This isn't funny." She poured them both mugs of coffee and handed him his, which he took with his left hand. "You've got to get out of here before there's more trouble."

"No way," he said, taking a sip of his coffee before setting the mug on the counter. "I'm a college professor now, not some wild-ass kid."

"Have it your way," Delia said, rewrapping the makeshift ice pack. "And don't say I didn't warn you."

"He shouldn't have talked to you like that." His lips grazed her neck and nibbled her earlobe. She smelled like Ivory soap. "When we were in high school," he whispered, "I used to hope that some-thing would happen—like your car would break down or there'd be a storm or something—and I'd be the one to help you out." He leaned closer, moving his mouth to her lips. "J. C. Brown would be a big hero, rescuing Saint Delia from drowning in the river or getting swept up in a tornado."

Her body softened against his. "I'm sorry I wasn't more accident-prone."

"Yeah," he whispered. "But it's never too late."

"I HATE TO BE the bearer of bad news," Annie began, a statement that Georgia knew could mean anything from tonight's supper plans being cancelled to tor-nado warnings. She held the phone closer to her ear and sat down in her favorite living room chair, the one closest to the window. That way she could see anyone who approached the front porch this af-ternoon. The outside thermometer read one-hundred and eight, hot even for Texas.

"I'm sitting down, if that helps," Georgia said, try-ing not to yawn. She hadn't slept well last night, even after working so late, because she'd seen Delia leave the fireworks with J. C. Brown.

"Well—"

"Don't get your pants in a bunch, Annie. I know Delia took off with the Brown boy last night." And she sure hoped her daughter knew what she was doing. Courting trouble, if anyone asked her, but of course no one had.

"It's not that, not exactly." Annie sighed. "J.C. was arrested for hitting Martin this morning."

"Hitting Martin? Whatever for? And Delia? What about *her*?"

"I think she's in love with him, Georgia."

"That's not what I meant." Though that possibility was bad enough. "Is Delia all right?"

"According to Bill Ripley's aunt—she's the one at Pecan Hollow—Martin showed up at Delia's this morning and—oh, dear, Georgia."

"He found J.C. there," Georgia finished for her. "I guess it was inevitable."

"Well, they sure looked intense last night, Georgia, out there on the dance floor. He's such a handsome man and—"

"Annie, what happened this *morning*?" Thank goodness for portable phones. She could walk over to the liquor cabinet and pour a little gin into her glass of lemonade without missing one second of the conversation. "Martin was jealous and made a scene?"

"Uh, not exactly. Betty told Bill's aunt that Julie broke up with Martin and he went over to Delia's after that and then I guess he flapped his mouth too much and wouldn't leave and J.C. belted him."

"This is sounding like a really bad soap opera," Georgia declared, taking a sip of her drink. She added a little more gin and then returned to her chair.

"I thought you'd be more upset." Annie sounded relieved. "Are you drinking?"

"Yes."

"Good."

"I don't mind Martin getting a punch in the nose," she confessed. "I would have liked to have done that to him myself after what he did to my daughter. Maybe J.C. is going to make himself useful after all."

"Hold on—I'm getting some tea."

"Put some whiskey in it, unless you want to come over here and drink gin."

"Too hot," Annie said, and Georgia heard ice cubes plunked into a glass. "I've got my air conditioner turned up high and I'm staying put in front of the TV."

"You don't want to bail my future son-in-law out of jail?" Annie didn't say anything, so Georgia continued, "If he's going to sleep with her, he should marry her. And then have children."

"What happened to Delia moving home?"

"I guess I'd better give it up and settle for grandchildren instead." She took another healthy swallow of her lemonade. "Don't you think?"

"He *was* awfully good with his niece and nephew. And his and Delia's babies would be terribly good-looking."

"Yes," Georgia said. "My thoughts exactly."

"I DON'T KNOW what was worse," Joe said, stepping out of his truck in front of Betty's trailer. "Getting tossed in jail or having your mother show up to bail me out."

"That was a shock," Delia admitted, waiting by

her car. Georgia had seemed almost disappointed to discover that Martin had dropped the charges, thanks to Julie's intervention, and Joe was about to leave the July police station without having needed Georgia's bail money.

"I haven't been arrested in years," Joe mused, seeming more casual about the whole mess than she thought normal. "And I never had so many people trying to get me out of jail as I did this afternoon."

"I'm sorry," she said, unwilling to follow him into the Brown home.

He gave her a quick kiss on the mouth. "I'm not. I'd hit him again."

"Don't say that."

Joe's smile faded. "I'll admit, sweetheart, that I'm looking forward to going home. You want to come with me? See the ranch? Meet the horses?"

She hesitated, unsure of the invitation. "Maybe," she said. "For a couple of days."

"Let's leave in the morning." He wrapped his arms around her as Hank opened the door, ran to greet them and wrapped his arms around their legs.

"Uncle Joe! Dee-yah!"

"Hey, kid." Joe released Delia and picked up his nephew. "I guess I'd better go inside and thank Julie for her help."

"I wonder what she promised Martin to get him to drop the charges and apologize to you."

"I don't want to know," he answered. "Are you going to bed early or can I come over later?"

"You can come over." She looked at him and winked. *You can sleep in my bed, too. Eventually.*

His smile proved he got the message.

12

"THIS IS the best thing that's happened all day," Delia said, rolling on top of Joe and leaning forward for his kiss. It was after ten on one of the hottest nights so far this summer, so they'd met after dinner and eaten ice cream from the carton in bed, the cool air-conditioned air making the trailer feel like the inside of a refrigerator.

"Damn right, sweetheart." His hands framed her face. "I think I've had enough of July for a while."

"I'm sorry." It had been the day-from-hell, starting with Martin's whining and ending—finally—with naked Joe, who wasn't whining at all. In fact, the man looked positively content with his life. His knuckles, still red and swollen, were the only reminders of this morning's mess.

"Quit saying that. It's not your fault I landed in jail. Besides," he said, smiling. "Your mother was actually nice to me. What was all that about? Did she ever tell you?"

"She'd been drinking."

"That explains it, then. I thought that friend of hers—"

"Annie," Delia supplied. He tasted like chocolate when she kissed him.

"Yeah. I thought Annie smelled a little like whiskey, but on a Saturday afternoon?"

"They're known to kick back a few, especially when they're worried about something." And her mother wouldn't have taken the news of Joe's arrest well. "I still don't understand why she went to the sheriff to have you bailed out."

"Maybe she's changed her mind about the Browns." His hand skimmed over her bare breasts. "Or maybe she liked the fact that your ex-husband got his nose broken."

"She muttered something about him to Sheriff Barker, but I didn't hear."

"She kept giving me very strange looks," Joe said.

"She thinks I'm falling in love with you." She couldn't believe those words had slipped out.

"Good. Because it damn well better be mutual."

"Meaning?" *He loves me?*

"Sweetheart, I've fallen so hard that I'm about half-crazy. So we're getting out of here first thing in the morning."

She wriggled against his erection. "First thing?"

"Second thing."

"After sex, after coffee, after—" She stopped talking when he lifted her hips and slid himself into her. She didn't know how anything could be so right, so perfect, so absolutely wonderful, but if this was love, then she was ready to enjoy every minute. So much for one-night stands.

Hours later, long after darkness overtook the trailer, Delia threw back the sheet and coughed. Somebody was burning trash, she thought sleepily. And the smell was seeping into the trailer.

"Yuk," she said aloud, sitting up and frowning. She rose to go to the bathroom, but a film of smoke stopped her from seeing the door.

"Joe? Joe!" She put her hand out and grabbed the doorjamb. The burning smell was coming from inside the trailer. She reached for the light switch, but the power didn't come on.

"What?"

"I think the trailer's on fire. There's smoke everywhere and it smells really bad." She heard him hurry toward her, then his hand grabbed her arm and pulled her to the floor.

"Stay low," he said. "We need to get out of here without breathing any of this."

"But we don't have any clothes—"

"Wait a sec." He rustled around the floor and came up with his T-shirt, which he handed to her. "Put that on."

"I don't see any fire," she said, pulling the shirt over her head. She heard him bang into the bed and figured he was finding something to put on. The smoke was getting thicker by the second, but Delia couldn't believe that there was really a fire. "Maybe it's some kind of weird electrical problem. I don't hear a fire."

"*Something's* wrong." He moved past her on his hands and knees. "Follow me. We're going to get out. Now."

"But my things—"

"Now," he said, grabbing her wrist to make her start crawling after him as the smoke detector in the kitchen started to beep.

She thought of her beads and books, Uncle Gin's guitars and the boxes of music she'd organized into notebooks. Everything could be lost if the place really was in danger of burning up. She coughed again, and hurried after Joe.

"Shit," he muttered. "It's getting worse. Stay down."

They needed wet cloths to put over their faces, she realized, but she didn't detour to get any as they crawled past the bathroom. After what seemed like an endless amount of time, Joe reached the kitchen door and pushed it open. Clean, hot air greeted them as soon as they tumbled out of the door and climbed down the warm steps.

"Now what?"

"Wait here," he said. "I'm going to call the fire department."

She watched as he sprinted across the road to Betty's. He wore nothing but white jockey shorts, but there was no one awake to see a mostly nude man running away from her smoking trailer in the middle of the night. She wondered where she'd left her cell phone, wished she had slept with underpants on, slapped mosquitoes as the smoke continued to puff from the open kitchen door.

There was still no sign of flames, but she knew that even without seeing fire, the firemen would douse the trailer with water and ruin everything. Joe disappeared into his mother's double-wide and she saw the lights come on before she crawled back inside to rescue the stack of notebooks on the kitchen table. It was harder to see than before, but she scrambled along the kitchen floor until she reached the table and grabbed the books.

"What the hell are you doing?"

"The songs," she gasped, tossing the books toward the door where Joe's voice came.

"It's not worth—oh, hell." He was behind her in seconds, helping her toss the books out the door, swearing when she tried to remove Gin's guitars from the wall above the couch. "Go," he said, his voice hoarse.

"But the guitars—"

"I'll get them. Get down and get *out*."

She did as he said, scurrying along the floor toward the door. A flashlight lit the way, spilling light from the outside.

"Are you okay?" Julie grabbed her hand and helped her down the stairs.

"Fine," she said, coughing a little as she turned to watch for Joe. "Joe?"

"Here." He appeared in the door and handed her the guitars. "Hurry and get back, both of you. It's getting worse in there."

Delia gave a guitar to Julie and retrieved the notebooks from the dirt.

"Toss them in your car and I'll drive it out of the way," Joe ordered. "The sooner we get out of here the better."

No one argued. Delia followed Julie across the street while Joe backed her car out of the driveway and parked it next to his truck. Delia watched in horror as flames shot out of the opened trailer door. "I can't believe this is happening."

"You two had better get some clothes on," Julie said when her brother joined them on the front lawn. "Here come the neighbors *and* the fire trucks."

Betty called to them from the front door. "Joseph? What's happening? And why don't you have any pants—oh, my goodness."

"You shouldn't ask a man that question," he said, walking toward the back door. "Not at three in the morning."

"Never mind," she said, as the fire trucks screamed into the park. "I'll get you both something to wear."

Delia looked down at the notebook she still clutched to her chest. A plastic-covered page had ripped and stuck out from the binder. She opened the book to stuff the page back inside when, from the light of Julie's flashlight, she read the title of the song: "I Used To Be On Fire, Now I'm Just Burning Down."

She didn't think she'd be singing that one anytime soon.

"You got to be a hero after all," Delia sniffed, wiping her nose on a tissue from the box she kept on her lap. Joe figured she'd been crying for about an hour now and he would do and say anything to get her to stop.

If he could think of anything.

"Joseph's always been good in a crisis," his mother said. They were sitting around the Browns' kitchen table. Now that the firemen were gone and the sun was up, nobody seemed to know what to do. The neighbors, still walking past the trailer to see the destruction, pointed and shook their heads, while inside Joe and his family wondered how to comfort the woman who'd lost her house and all of her possessions.

"It doesn't take a genius to get out of a smoking building," he pointed out. Joe wanted nothing more than to take Delia in his arms and carry her out of the room to a bed. She looked exhausted, despite the coffee she'd been drinking for hours. Georgia, called at dawn by her daughter, had arrived at high speed an hour ago.

"Did they say—"

"The air conditioner probably. It was as old as the

trailer and the wiring was faulty. At least that's what the fire chief said."

"Oh. The switch was turned off when I moved in." Delia wiped her eyes again. "We turned it back on because of the heat."

"And the smell," Georgia said. "Don't forget that."

"The old man likely didn't run the air conditioning much," Betty pointed out. "He sure didn't seem to feel the heat."

"Yes," Georgia agreed. "He said the sun made his bones feel better, that if folks couldn't take the heat they should move to Alaska."

"Maybe I should move to Alaska then." Her mother handed Delia a fresh cup of coffee.

"Come home for a few days first." Georgia patted her shoulder. "Before you make any decisions about your future."

"What about your old house?" Julie met her brother's raised eyebrows. "Well? It's still her house until Martin sells it."

"No, thanks." Delia picked up her coffee mug and turned around to look out the window at the remains of her trailer. "Who would think something made of metal would burn up like that?"

"It didn't exactly burn up," Georgia said. "'Melted' might be a better word."

"At least no one was hurt," Betty added.

"Fire truck," Hank crowed, showing off one of last year's Christmas presents. Joe made sure the truck didn't land on the kitchen table and scooped the child onto the chair next to his.

"Yeah," he said. "That's a fire truck, all right. Don't hit anyone with it, buddy."

"'Kay." Hank clutched the truck to his chest.

"At least I got Uncle Gin's music out safe."

"That's something," Georgia agreed, but her expression clearly showed that she didn't see a reason to celebrate.

"I really liked that trailer. It was the first place that belonged just to me." Delia looked down at the clothes she wore: Joe's T-shirt along with Julie's underpants and denim maternity shorts. "I'm going to have to go shopping."

"Good idea," said Georgia, standing up and picking up her purse. "That will cheer you up. Come home now and take a shower."

Julie nodded. "You can take any of my clothes that you want, Delia."

"Seeing how you took her husband," Georgia said, "I guess that's a fair enough trade."

"Ignore her," Delia said. "My mother has never been tactful."

To Joe's surprise, Betty laughed. "Well, isn't that the truth! Georgia, you've always said what you meant, no matter what. I wish I had that kind of nerve."

Delia's mother looked intrigued. "If you did, what would you say?"

Betty smiled. "I'd tell you to mind your manners and start acting nicer to my children."

"Point taken. Delia? Put that tissue box down and get a grip on yourself. Losing Gin's trailer isn't the end of the world. Nobody died. You can buy more clothes and more beads and more books. Come home with me and clean up."

"I'll take her to town later, Mrs. Ball." Joe decided that it was time he put Delia back to bed. "She can rest here for a while."

"But—"

"The stores aren't going to open for hours, so I'll come home later." Delia took Joe's hand and got to her feet. "I think I'd rather go to bed with Joe now." She blushed. "I mean, I think I'll go lie down. Alone."

He leaned over and whispered, "I liked it the first way."

"Shh."

He led her down the hall after she'd say goodbye to everyone. He tucked her into his bed and covered her with an ivory sheet. "Are you going to be okay?"

"Sure." Her smile was a little wobbly. "This is just a temporary setback to my life of independence."

"Speaking of your life," Joe began, wishing he could come up with a better way to say this. "Why don't you start it over in Austin? With me."

"I never thought about moving to Austin," she said. "I'd like to see your ranch, though."

"And I intend to show it to you." He took a deep breath and brushed the hair from her cheek. "Marry me, Delia. I know this is fast, but the fire—well, what

the hell? I think I've loved you for a long time. And
I know I'm in love with you now. Why wait?"

"Marry you," she repeated, looking at him with
huge eyes. "Just like that?"

"If that's too fast, then move in with me. Leave
July and don't look back. We'll live together and plan
the rest of our lives. We'll drive out of here the way
we'd planned."

"You make it sound so simple."

"It is. You need a place to live," Joe said, teasing
her with his lips on hers. "Why not with me?"

She shook her head. "I can't marry you because I
need a place to live."

"Sure you can." He grinned. "Unless you plan to
move home with your mother."

"Ouch."

"Sleep on it." He kissed her. "And then say yes."

DELIA SAID NO. She'd thought there would be no way
she could sleep after losing her home and getting a
marriage proposal, but she'd finally napped in Joe's
bed when everything became too overwhelming to
think about.

And then, hours later, she'd said no, because she
was scared of making another mistake. No, because
she didn't want him to regret such an impulsive proposal. And no, because she didn't want to use marriage as an easy way out.

Delia was unprepared for the hurt that flashed
across Joe's face.

"Can I ask why?"

"It's not you," she said. "It's me."

"Right." His hands gripped the steering wheel of her car, parked in along the street in front of her mother's imposing home. He looked straight ahead, as if something down the street was so interesting he couldn't tear his gaze away. "You want to explain that?"

"I've only been divorced a few months," she began, wondering how to make him understand. "I need more time—"

"Yeah," he said. "You want to walk on the wild side a while longer, I guess. Take home a few more men, dance in a few more bars, drink a few more frozen daiquiris?"

"That's not it and you know it."

He turned to look at her again. "You were in a dead-end marriage for years. How much more time do you want to waste?"

"I want to see if I can survive on my own."

"We can all survive on our own," Joe said. "The question is, why would we want to?"

"I don't want people feeling sorry for me."

"Too late, sweetheart. Your husband left you and your trailer just burned down. Folks are revvin' up major sympathy as we speak."

Well, that was blunt. And true. The temptation to run to Joe's ranch in Austin grew stronger, but Delia was determined. Her only attempt at independence had resulted in a fire, so obviously she had a ways to go before becoming self-sufficient. "I'm not going to visit you," she added. "Not yet. Not until I'm sure."

He swore. And kissed her goodbye.

Then, looking more resigned than irritated, he said, "I hope you do whatever it is you need to do, Delia. I've waited since I was sixteen, but I'm not going to wait forever."

He left her there. He slid out of the car, refused her offer to drive him to the school to retrieve his truck from the parking lot, and headed down the street. He didn't look back, not that Delia expected him to. And as she unloaded her meager possessions from the back seat of her car, she told herself that this was all for the best.

But she suspected this was going to be a very long summer.

POOR DELIA, folks said while eating their eggs and bacon at the Yellow Rose Diner Saturday morning. That girl had some bad luck, all right, but that old trailer of her uncle's wasn't worth much. At least Delia could live with her mother now.

How sad about Delia, neighbors said to Betty Brown when they came to play cards. Such a shame to have lost her company in Pecan Hollow and had Betty's son heard from her? After all, they made such a nice couple together.

Poor Delia, Lily May said as she curled Georgia's hair two weeks later. Hard to believe she took up with J. C. Brown, who dumped her right after the fire. That girl has the worst luck with men, the hairdresser pointed out. And why on earth was Delia living in rooms above the Sew Good craft shop on Main Street?

Georgia sniffed, resisting a retort that would give Lily May something to gossip about for the rest of the summer. "She's working there, of course," she found the patience to say. "She gives lessons in beading— my Delia's quite the artist, you know—and she runs the place for Ethel, who wants to retire and spend more time with her grandchildren."

"A bead artist?" Lily May frowned into the mirror as if she'd never heard of such a thing. "That sounds awful strange."

Georgia announced that Delia's last Victorian-style purse had sold for an enormous sum, the "price of a new truck", she said. A downright lie, but worth the telling if only to make the hairdresser shut her mouth.

"My, my, who knew," Lily May clucked. "Maybe she can afford to buy herself a nice house now that Martin sold that big one they had."

"I don't know what she's going to do next," Georgia said, and that was the truth. She told Annie the same thing later, when they met at the café for lunch. "She's not happy, Annie."

"She misses that man, of course," Annie whispered. "You know who."

"I know. I thought the money Martin finally gave her would cheer her up, but other than taking some of her money worries away, it didn't seem to make much difference." They ordered chicken salad plates and iced tea before Georgia continued. "I wonder what happened. Here I had my hopes up and everything, but Delia won't say anything except that he went back to Austin."

"Betty might know. Call her and ask."

"I can't just call her and ask why her son left my daughter."

"But I can."

She watched as Annie pulled a tiny cell phone out of her quilted tote bag. "When did you get that?"

"The kids gave it to me. For emergencies."

"Well, if this isn't one I don't know what is."

"Darn right," Annie said. "Go ask Greta for a phone book and we'll be in business."

"SURPRISE!"

Delia looked up from unpacking a box of knitting pattern books and saw her mother entering the store. It had been a long, quiet day, with only five minutes left until closing, so she was ridiculously happy to see her. Georgia waved some papers in her hand and smiled.

"Hi, Mother. What are you so excited about?"

"You'll be excited, too, when I tell you." Georgia hurried over to the counter and plopped a glossy brochure on top of instructions on how to knit a sweater for a dog. "Remember that trip we talked about a few months ago, right after you moved into Gin's trailer?"

"Vaguely." She'd been too consumed with lust for Joe Brown at the time to pay much attention. "Maybe you'd better remind me."

"The *cruise*," her mother explained, pointing to a photograph of a large white ship plowing through blue water. "We sail out of Galveston and on to Mexico and all those wonderful ruins."

"I can't go on a cruise," she said, waving her arm around the cluttered shelves of the craft store. "Ethel depends on me."

"I already talked to her and she gave you the twelve days off as a special favor to me." Georgia's cheeks were pink with excitement. "Isn't that wonderful?"

"Um." Wonderful would not be the word she would choose to describe going on a cruise for twelve days with her mother. With Joe? She'd swim to the ship. But he hadn't called her since he left and that had been two months and twelve days ago. He would have started school by now. He'd be teaching those young, gorgeous tanned women—

"Annie's going, too, of course." Now her mother pulled something else out of her purse. "Ta-da! Here are the reservations and information we need. One night is very elegant, so we have to dress up. We'll go shopping together on your next day off."

"Mother, I don't know what to say." Surely going on a cruise with her mother and her mother's best friend shouldn't rank up there on the scale of misery with a divorce and a house fire, but Delia felt a familiar knot of misery in her stomach. The same knot that tightened its grip every time she thought of Joe and wondered what he was doing. If he missed her. If he thought about coming back to July and making love with her all night long.

"You don't have to say anything, Delia." The papers returned to her handbag. "Just be ready to go in two weeks from Saturday."

"But—"

"Oh, this will be the first of many trips we'll take now that you're single and carefree. We'll have lots of fun together, I just know it. You'll see that the divorce was a good thing, and so was ending that thing you had going on with the Brown boy. Oh, he was a handsome thing, but as you get older you'll realize that all that physical business is vastly overrated."

Delia opened her mouth to say something—anything—but no words came out.

Georgia pushed the brochure toward her. "Keep it to look at tonight when you're upstairs having dinner. That's what Annie and I do." She left as quickly as she entered, the bell on the door tinkling as she shut it behind her. Delia hurried over to lock the door, hang the Closed sign and draw the shades.

She had news to share, too, but the person she wanted to share it with was in Austin. Talking to beautiful coeds. All she had right now were two guitars, five binders of really sad songs, a reservation on a cruise ship and a letter from a music publisher.

Somewhere, somehow, her life had gone terribly

wrong. *My Life Has Gone Terribly Wrong*. Sounded like one of Uncle Gin's song titles.

J.C. CURSED the heat, the traffic and the meeting that led to his leaving his air-conditioned office and negotiating the heavy Friday afternoon traffic downtown. His temper had grown increasingly short, his patience deteriorating as the weeks without Delia wore on.

He'd kept busy. He'd assured himself that he'd change her mind. He'd told himself he'd give her until Thanksgiving. Halloween, maybe, if he got desperate. He could last another five or six weeks without going crazy.

Maybe.

He parked in a garage near Sixth Street, the music hub of Texas, if not the world. And he wondered for the hundredth time why he had to meet Julie in the first place. She could have talked to him on the phone. Or in his office. Or even out at the ranch. But no, leave it to her to be mysterious and demanding. He walked the four blocks to The Blue Door and stepped inside. The place, dark and cool, was nearly empty except for a handful of college kids at a table by the front door and a couple of old men on bar stools. The band was setting up on a stage in the corner.

He was early and, now that he was here, he didn't mind waiting. He ordered a beer and sat down at the far end of the bar to take his time drinking it.

He heard a woman order a strawberry daiquiri and the memory made him smile despite his aggravation.

"I know you," the woman said, perching on the stool next to him. "From high school." The hairs on the back of his neck stood up and he turned to see Delia sitting beside him. She wore a white sundress that bared her shoulders, emphasized her cleavage and showed off her legs. It was a dress meant to drive him crazy, he realized, and it was working.

"Yeah?" He couldn't hide his smile.

"I let you copy the answers off my math paper."

"And I appreciated it." She wasn't the only one who remembered how they'd met at the Cottonwood. The bartender set the drink in front of her and Joe paid for it before she could pull her wallet from her purse. "Julie set me up, didn't she."

"She owed me a favor."

"Yeah." He took a swallow of beer and tried not to get his hopes up too high. "This is a real nice surprise and all, but are you going to tell me what are you doing here?"

"I had business in Austin," she said, which was not the answer he wanted to hear. "Successful business with a music publisher who's interested in old country songs like Uncle Gin's." She smiled wide enough to light up the room. "Those songs we saved from the fire could turn out to be worth a small fortune. He's already made me an offer and I'm going to get an agent before I accept it."

"Congratulations." And he meant it, too. But he

didn't want her to be here, with him, just because she'd had to be in Austin on business.

"Quit frowning. I came here to see you, too."

"Are you going to get drunk like last time we were in a bar together?"

"No." She smiled at him. "But I've missed you so much that I'll still let you take me home."

"Home?"

"To your place. If I'm still invited."

"I guess that depends on how long you're staying." He fought to keep from pulling her into his arms, but it wasn't easy.

"I guess that depends on how long I'm invited to stay."

"Oh, you can stay as long as you want," he told her. "Getting married would, of course, be my first option, but I'm more open-minded now, looking at you in that dress. I'd even be happy for a couple of hours of your time."

"Is that a proposal?" He swore she looked as if she was about to cry.

"Yeah," he admitted. "But I've been so damn miserable that I'll admit that I'll take what I can get."

"'Being alone is vastly overrated,'" Delia agreed. "I'm quoting my mother now, but she's right."

He nodded solemnly. "You must be losing your mind."

"And my heart, too," she said. "Losing my mind, losing my heart, all because of losing you."

Joe laughed. "Uncle Gin?"

"His next greatest hit. You know," she whispered, leaning closer so he got a good look at the tops of her breasts. "This is the most amazing piece of clothing. When I untie the straps at the nape of my neck, the whole dress just peels right off."

Joe couldn't take any more. He slid off the bar stool, took her hand and her outside into the bright sun. Parked in front of the bar was Delia's white Cadillac. And hitched to Delia's white Cadillac was an older-model Silverstream trailer.

"Like it? I bought it with the money I got when the house sold. It's my workshop," she proudly announced. "What do you think?"

"You goin' somewhere, sweetheart?"

She looped her arms around his waist, causing more than a few tourists to stare. "Out to your place, of course. I thought I'd park it at your place—"

"*Our* place," he corrected, which made her smile again.

"And use it as my studio. I've registered for art classes next semester." She put her nose against his shirt and inhaled. "I love the way you smell."

"Would you like to have wild and crazy sex with me?"

"That was my line," Delia protested, looking up to laugh. Joe paused a second before he kissed her.

"And," he promised, "it will be a cold day in July before I turn down an offer like that from you again."

Epilogue

"LISTEN TO THIS," Georgia said, holding the *July Times* in front of her. Annie leaned closer. "'The wedding of Delia Ball Drummond, daughter of Mrs. Georgia Ball and the late Richard Ball, to Mr. Joseph Carter Brown, son of Mrs. Elizabeth Brown, took place Saturday, July fourth, on the groom's ranch in Austin.'"

"It was a lovely wedding," Annie agreed, taking tissues from her purse because she knew that her best friend was going to get weepy again. Just mention the word "wedding" and Georgia turned into a fountain. "Everyone said so. And Joe's sister was so sweet. Not at all like I'd pictured her."

"She's cleaned up her act, learned how to knit and quit drinking. I think Delia was a good influence. She got her a job at Sew Good, remember." She looked down at the newspaper again. "'The happy couple will reside on their ranch in Austin after a honeymoon in San Antonio.'" Georgia set the paper on the counter and looked around the Yellow Rose as if waiting for congratulations. Two women waved and the waitress ignored them. "I offered to give them a cruise, but they said no."

"Speaking of cruises," Annie began. "Did you ever tell her?"

Georgia chuckled. "That I never booked her on a cruise with us? Of course not, though I sure would like to take credit for pushing her back into Joe's arms."

"Betty had a lovely time, even if she couldn't climb the steps to the top of that pyramid in Xtapa. But she took some good pictures of us waving from the top."

"I'd like to see Martin's face when he reads about the wedding. He's stuck in that condo of his with his son—did I tell you Karl's pregnant girlfriend is living there, too?" Annie nodded. She'd heard all about the stepson who couldn't find a job and had come home to July to live off his father. "And Jen is home, too," Georgia continued, "because the little snob flunked out of school. Martin has a houseful."

Annie watched her friend's face dissolve into tears. "Georgia, what's the matter?"

"Oh, Annie, I'm so happy." She took the tissue and wiped her eyes. "You were right all along, you know."

"About what?"

"That Delia's still young enough to give me grand-children." She sighed and another round of tears creased her cheeks.

"So J. C. Brown turned out to be a pretty decent man after all," Annie pointed out, tickled that Georgia would have her own baby pictures to show at future card games.

"Joe," Georgia corrected. "His name is Joe."

* * * * *

*Look for more BOOTS & BOOTIES
coming in October 2004!
Popular author Kristine Rolofson delivers*
Made in Texas. *Enjoy!*

On sale now

girls' night in

21 of today's hottest
female authors
1 fabulous short-story collection
And all for a good cause.

Featuring *New York Times* bestselling authors

Jennifer Weiner (author of *Good in Bed*),
Sophie Kinsella (author of *Confessions of a Shopaholic*),
Meg Cabot (author of *The Princess Diaries*)

Net proceeds to benefit War Child, a network of organizations
dedicated to helping children affected by war.

Also featuring bestselling authors...

Carole Matthews, Sarah Mlynowski, Isabel Wolff, Lynda Curnyn,
Chris Manby, Alisa Valdes-Rodriguez, Jill A. Davis, Megan McCafferty,
Emily Barr, Jessica Adams, Lisa Jewell, Lauren Henderson,
Stella Duffy, Jenny Colgan, Anna Maxted, Adèle Lang,
Marian Keyes and Louise Bagshawe

www.RedDressInk.com   www.WarChildusa.org

Available wherever trade paperbacks are sold.

™ is a trademark of the publisher.
The War Child logo is the registered trademark of War Child.

RDIGNIMMR